Most Wanted

Vol.15 of Indian Creek Anthology Series

Most Wanted
Volume 15 of the Indian Creek Anthology Series

Published by Southern Indiana Writers, 2200 Reno Ave., New Albany, IN, 47150
            or   2868 Alonzo Smith Rd., Georgetown, IN 47122

Book designed by T. Lee Harris

ISSN 1085-357X
ISBN 978-0-578-01670-2

Cover design by T. Lee Harris

Photograph by Yesteryear Tintype Old Time Photos, Nashville, IN

Contents

Seventh Son

by

Ginny Fleming

Crickets vied with exotic nightbirds to own the darkness surrounding the huge old house. Barely visible in the Colombian mountain's cool, foggy foothills, its lines hinted at old-money status. A full moon grinned down from a cloudless sky, passing judgment on the night, sailing on its nightly voyage across the inky heavens.

The house sat on a hillside like a live thing; a moonlit road leading up to the estate curved around the hill. Like a great cat awaiting the arrival of its prey; curling its tail around its haunches, it hungered.

The waiting over, a four-wheeled drive Jeep slowly made its way up the hill, maneuvering around the stones and numerous potholes impeding its progress. Finally having conquered the difficult road, and torturing the hand brake until it squealed into submission, the driver pulled the vehicle to a stop in front of the mysterious house.

Before climbing out of the Jeep, the man carefully checked over a blanket-wrapped bundle laid across the back seat. Satisfied with the bundle's condition, he quietly shut and locked the auto's rugged door and hurried the few feet to the house.

After rapping the massive door's heavy knocker, the red-haired bearded man once again furtively glanced over his shoulder as if fearing he might be observed. A second rapping brought an answer in the form of a small peephole sliding open, and the man realized he was being scrutinized from behind the door.

"Jonathan Randal. Is Señor Delgado in? He's expecting me."

As the door swung open on its hesitant hinges, the resulting squeaks and groans reminded Randal of the horror movies he'd watched as a child. He shuddered in spite of himself, entering the darkened foyer, half expecting to be greeted by Dracula himself.

Instead, Randal looked up into the dark eyes of a beautiful woman. The feminine vision's long golden blond hair tumbled luxuriously over her shoulders to her waist. Fighting an inane impulse to stand nose to nose with the statuesque female for confirmation, Randal estimated she was taller than himself by a head. *Whoa, Baby! Walk me down old funky street; Lord knows I feel good enough to eat!*

5

. . . I hope I'm not drooling! He silently shook his head with bewilderment, wondering what perverse part of his brain originated *that* inappropriately lustful thought. An inner hysteric reminded the man his mission was urgent; he *couldn't* allow himself to be distracted by a beautiful woman.

"My husband will see you now," the Latin woman sadly replied, "and may God help us all." As she led him to a room down a long hallway, Randal's eyes unconsciously followed the sultry sway of the woman's curvaceous hips. Dressed in a white lacy blouse and a long flowing semi-transparent yellow skirt, every step she took caused the soft material to rustle softly each time her hips rocked from side to side. He listened to the music of her silver reptile-skinned boots' heels as they clicked on the inlaid tile floor, and as he followed close behind, Randal caught a faint wafting perfume coming back to his nostrils.

Yes, he commented to himself, *this Delgado character is purported to be many things, but he surely is a lucky man!*

She brought Randal to the door, indicating he should knock before entering, then, with a fluid sensual motion the golden-haired beauty crossed herself before hurrying out of sight.

"These Latin types sure are melodramatic," Randal muttered, raising his hand to knock.

A voice called through the door: "Come in" and Randal entered, shutting the door quietly behind himself. This room was a sharp contrast to the foyer and hallway in that it was brightly lit, causing Randal to squint momentarily. As his daylight vision came to him, the man soon noted a huge desk dominated the room. A massive ox-blood leather swivel chair sat behind the desk, its occupant hidden, turned to the wall.

A voice emanated from the cordovan chair in a thick Colombian accent. "So, Señor Randal, atheist, bigot, skeptic, television pit-bull and world famous debunker of the supernatural; you have *finally* found your way to my door. What kept you? I wish you to know that I have no fear of your American talk-show journalism. I am simply a man with a gift from God; and by your call it appears you find yourself in need of my services."

This statement earned the disembodied voice a raised eyebrow from Jonathan Randal.

7

The thick accented voice continued, "If I were not a *compassionate* man, I might find that very amusing. Usually at this time, I would say that I'm pleased to make your acquaintance, but should I allow myself that pleasantry... I would be lying."

Randal allowed himself a subtle snort; he'd heard it all before. He wasn't called the American Pit-Bull for nothing, and he wasn't running for "Miss Congeniality".

Again the voice spoke. "Allow me to say I am merely curious to meet you. But, where are my manners? Please have a seat. Make yourself comfortable and tell me of your plight."

Pulling a richly upholstered fireside chair up to the desk, Randal sat down. The massive red-leather chair swiveled to face him, revealing a small man dressed all in white, smiling from across the desk at the momentarily startled American.

"Señor, allow me to introduce myself," the small dark-haired man said with obvious amusement. "I am Miguel Delgado. I *am* the Seventh Son of the Seventh Son—"

"As the old song says," Randal interrupted, regaining his composure, "you can heal the sick, raise the dead— make'a little girls talk outta their head, right?"

"Yes . . . I can do that . . . and more." Delgado laughed. Rising up from the chair, he came out from behind the desk. "Would you care for a drink, Señor Randal?"

"I don't care for that tequila you guys drink down here. At least, not the kind with the worm in it." The red-bearded American made a rude face.

Delgado threw back his head and laughed deeply. "Neither do I, Señor Randal, neither do I. It is a common fallacy of North Americanos that we Colombians are all muy macho banditos. I much prefer good Kentucky Bourbon. Join me? Bueno."

The diminutive man easily reached the amber-colored bottle on the side-board, pouring two whiskeys over the ice cubes he fished from a golden ice bucket. "My wife doesn't like for me to drink, Señor Randal— but a man must have his drink, otherwise, what is life, eh?"

Randal took the offered glass. The American toasted: "Vivá Felecidad!"

"Live long and prosper, Spock," a slyly smiling Delgado replied.

The red-haired man took a healthy swallow in honor of his host while thinking to himself: *This is definitely the best Kentucky bourbon. Whoa! It slid down my throat as smooth as silk slides over a whore's ass!*

As he savored the fine liquor's warm burning sensation, the American looked around the room. It seemed to be a study of sorts. Filled bookcases made up two sides of the room, a stereo system graced one wall, a mega-screen television commanded the other wall. *The fog must have concealed an expensive satellite dish— Hell, I'll bet he can pick up Japan's Funniest Home Videos!* Multiple photographs of the tall woman who answered the door adorned any surface that would hold a frame. *Something about these photos gives me an uncomfortable feeling. . . .*

An elaborately-framed photograph hanging by the window showed the woman standing arm in arm with a tall dark-haired man. Both were smiling, dressed completely in white, flowers woven into their hair. Randal wondered silently if this was a wedding photo. *If it is,* thought Randal, *then it must be her first husband . . . curiouser and curiouser.*

Without realizing it, the red-haired man leaned forward in his chair, hoping to get a better look at the picture. Randal's trained TV journalist's eye focused in on a strong resemblance between the tall man in the photo and Delgado, who stood before him; all three feet four inches. *Make a note of this,* Randal told himself. *I've got to sign this woman for a show about Women Who Marry Brothers. Women Who Marry Twins. Women Who Marry . . . Oh, to hell with it. I'm sure Oprah has covered it all before.*

"Ah, I see you recognize my wife from the pictures." Delgado smiled, picking up a framed photo from the front of his desk and carrying it with him as he climbed back into the massive chair. "Carmen is the light of my life. The sun rises every morning simply to get a glimpse of her. Her beauty is food for my soul—"

"Yeah, yeah, yeah, Delgado. She is *very* lovely. But, I didn't come here to ogle your wife." He finished his drink in a second swallow and sat the wet glass down on the desk's dark wood. Instinctively, a diabolic smirk crossed Randal's face, as he silently noted that without a coaster he'd leave one hell of a ring on the expensive surface, and the arrogant American knew he didn't give a damn. Out of habit, he snarled the words, "I have more urgent matters to discuss with you."

"Of course, Señor Randal," the miniature man smiled. He placed his hands together, fingers touching in a "church-steeple" fashion. "You must have a great need to seek out my service."

"Well, I see there's no reason to introduce myself to *you*, Delgado." Randal's words took on a huffy tone, "My reputation precedes me. But, let me add one thing to that lovely list of yours; I'm a desperate man. I've risked everything to come here. If it were known I've come to the Seventh Son for any reason but to show you up, I'd be laughed off the air. We both know it." The red-headed American halted momentarily, cleared his throat, and resumed in a much quieter tone, "Yes . . . we both know it . . . but, I've heard you have great healing power, as I've also heard there is a great price to pay for that power. Let me assure you, I'm prepared to pay your price. I'm *desperate* enough to tell you that up front."

A devilish smile played across Delgado's lips, and the dark-haired bantam-sized man released a laugh, a harsh stuttering laugh which sounded machine-like in its report. "A man... a man such as yourself, Señor Randal, would find the price too dear. Sometimes a service such as mine requires a piece of the *soul* as payment, and I'm afraid, Señor, you simply may come up wanting."

Delgado watched in wary amazement for the same reason a small mongoose might track the deadly dance of a huge cobra. The famous "Randal Pit-Bull Temper" unleashed itself into the body that just scant moments before sat somewhat calmly before him.

Randal rose to his feet towering above Delgado and slammed both fists onto the desk, rattling the remaining ice cubes in the glasses. "Are you saying, *little man*," Randal growled in a low, carefully modulated voice, made much more frightening by the obvious anger being held forcibly in check behind a rictus of a smile— some people having seen this smile later swore they gazed upon the visage of Satan himself. "Are you saying, you phony *little voo-doo man,* you think that I— *I*—Jonathan Randal— can't *get the money?!?* "

Somehow concealing his fear, the miniature man in the massive chair remained calm. Peaking his fingers again, he explained to the angry American as if speaking to a temperamental child. "Money? Oh, no. My friend, I have no doubt of your *ability* to pay *my* price. It's God's payment you may find yourself lacking."

Having to physically direct his frustrated anger somewhere, Randal unleashed an unholy howl and again hit the desk with both fists, jarring the room, before nearly throwing himself back into his chair in impotent frustration. "Delgado," he nearly screamed, *"what in the Hell* are you talking about?!?"

Delgado sighed. "It is of no consequence to you, Señor Randal. For you see, to be given a gift such as mine— a gloriously terrible gift, if it be known— I, also, must make a payment to God. And to be bluntly honest, Jonathan Randal, you are simply not worthy of my sacrifice." Delgado smiled and took a sip of his bourbon, placing the glass on the desktop blotter between what he hoped would pass for unshaking hands, before continuing nonchalantly as if discussing the weather. "Don't think for a moment I do not realize by refusing you I am bringing the wrath of your American Television Witch-Hunt Journalism down upon my head. How do you say in America— What, me worry? I do hope you have enjoyed your travels in my country. Might I suggest you visit the ruins before you leave? They are —"

"It's not for me."

"They are. . . Forgive me— Did you say something, Señor Randal?"

"I said, Mr. Delgado, it's not for myself," Randal replied in a soft and sad tone. "I came to you for . . . my little girl. She's asleep out in the car. We've come a long way . . . we've flown all day and she's exhausted. Lately, she's been so frail and—"

"Bring her in."

"Pardon me?"

"Bring her in, Señor Randal." The sarcastic smile disappeared from Delgado's lips and the amusement fled from his eyes. "I am not such a monster I would refuse a child; and I can plainly see you are not quite the monster you profess to be, either."

Carmen Delgado hovered near, as Randal gently laid his child, still wrapped in her fluffy pink blanket, on the overstuffed leather couch in her husband's study. "Miguel, you must not do this thing! You must not—" the tall woman begged, falling to her knees in front of the small man, blocking his path. "Please, my husband, for the love of God, you *cannot* do this thing!"

"Carmen . . . my darling— my life. . . ." Delgado kissed her palms one after the other, ending with a lingering kiss on her full red lips. His hand gently brushed a tear from her eye as he whispered lovingly, "I must. You know in your heart, *I must.* To refuse this child— Carmalita— would be to lose my soul."

"But, Miguel, it could cost you your life . . . your *life.* . . ."

"Better my life, dear one, than the life of this innocent child." He gently pushed Carmen aside and stepped up to the couch. Pulling the blanket back from the sleeping girl's face, Delgado estimated the child to be between four or five years of age. Although he wouldn't swear to it, he thought the illness *might* have made her appear to be younger. With a gentle touch, he smoothed her bright red hair from her sweat-beaded, fevered forehead, causing the little girl to awaken.

Bright blue eyes stared up into the face of the small man. "Hello," the child said shyly. "Are you one of Santa Claus' elves?"

Delgado smiled and gently patted her flushed cheek. Usually, this was not a question he'd smile about. "No, Chiquita Mia. I am not one of Saint Nicholas' elves; but I do work for his boss. I hear from your Papa that you are not feeling very well. That makes me very sad. Your Papa brought you here so I could make you well again. Would you like that?"

The little girl whispered, "Are you a doctor?"

"In a way, Chiquita. Some say I am a doctor of the soul." Delgado took the little girl's hands into his own and looked towards Randal standing beside the arm of the couch. "Señor Randal, I must ask you, are you prepared to meet the price of God?"

"How can you look into her face and ask me that, Delgado?" Randal lowered his head and kneeled beside the child. "If I even *have* a soul it belongs to Melody; without her I'm a walking dead man. Her mother's been gone— dead— for two years and Melody is all that I have left in this world. Please, I'm *begging* you to help her."

"As you wish, Señor Randal." Delgado placed Melody's tiny hands to his lips and whispered something Randal found incomprehensible. "Melody, Bambina Mia, I must unbutton the top of your nightgown. Is that all right with you? I promise I won't hurt you, but I must take the bad thing out of your body. Do you trust me, Chiquita? Your Papa wishes me to take the bad thing from your body because he loves you and wants you to feel better."

The little girl nodded her permission, and Delgado gently unbuttoned the first three buttons of the child's nightgown, revealing the translucent skin covering Melody's quivering chest. "Now, Bambina, this will feel like a little pinch. You are a brave girl. Yes, I can see you are." The dark-haired man closed his eyes and traced his right hand index finger down the little girl's sternum, stopping when he came to the end of her breastbone. Pausing there, he rubbed his finger back and forth as if attempting to rub some dirt from her skin. An audible "pop" sounded and Delgado's finger broke through the little girl's chest. Blood seeped slowly around Delgado's hand. He fished in the wound for what seemed to Randal to be month-long minutes.

Randal drew his breath in sharply. He could hardly believe what he was seeing— this man had his hand inside his daughter's chest! Randal's mind screamed for him to take action— to grab the little man away from Melody— to protect his daughter— but his body *refused* to move.

With a deep growl emanating from his throat, Delgado pulled his hand from the hole in Melody's chest. There, crawling across the diminutive man's hand was a tiny pink creature resembling a newly-born mouse.

Randal watched in terrified amazement while the mouse-like object squirmed and wriggled around Delgado's hand leaving a thin bloody trail down the life-line of the diminutive Colombian. Soon, the writhing death-crawl come to an end, the embryonic mouse-creature settled into place like it had found a life-giving teat, rooted and seemingly burrowed into his quivering palm. Delgado opened his mouth in what was first a silent scream. Seconds later, an agonizing wail pierced the air and the pink creature disappeared completely under the little man's skin.

His hand trembled. Delgado again reached down and rubbed the child's chest with his finger. The bleeding stopped when he closed the wound. As if by pulling an invisible zipper, he brought the skin together with his finger. Then with a weary sigh the dark-haired man again took the little girl's tiny hands in his own, touching her hands to his lips.

Suddenly a faint blue glow formed around the small man's lips and it flowed down the frail arms of the child. The eerie blue light reached Melody's face, and she cried out as if in pain.

"What have I done?" Kneeling on the floor beside the exotic woman, Randal roughly grabbed Carmen by the shoulders. He shrieked in anguish, "My God! What have I done— *he's killing her!!*"

"Dios Mio, you damned fool!" Carmen angrily spat out the words, ripping Randal's hands from her shoulders and pushing the hysterical man away. Tears streamed down her face matting her long blond hair to her cheeks. "Are you so blind you cannot see it's *him* he is killing? Your daughter will be fine. Damn you! *Your daughter will be fine!*"

Very soon, the blue light completely encompassed the little girl and Delgado. They both writhed in agony. Seconds later, an invisible switch flicked off. Melody and the little man each moaned a ragged sigh like a great burden was lifted from them both. Abruptly, Delgado's eyes rolled back into his head. He dropped the little girl's hands and fell to the floor in a faint.

"Miguel!!" Carmen screamed as she slid on her hands and knees across the floor to the couch. Cradling Delgado's head in her lap, she let her teardrops mingle between her fingers. Stroking her husband's hair, she smoothed his long dark curls away from his face. "Miguel, querido," she whispered, "what have you done?"

Randal asked quietly, "Will he be all right?"

Carmen slowly nodded her head. "For now. Yes, he will be all right." Gently kissing her husband's cheek, almost as if she feared awakening him, she hissed, "But, by all that is holy, he must *never* do this again. Please— Señor Randal— will you help me get him off of the floor and into his chair?"

Randal carefully picked up the small man from the floor and carried him across the room, placing him sideways in the chair. Carmen knelt beside the swivel chair, holding her breath until Delgado's eyelids moved and he slowly came to himself.

". . . Carmen, dear one," Miguel Delgado whispered weakly. "All is well." The dark-haired man smiled at his lovely wife. "How is Melody?"

As if hearing her name mentioned from across the room, the little girl stirred from her swoon, calling out in a faint voice, "Daddy . . . Daddy? Where are you?"

"Yes, Baby Girl! Daddy's here!" The Pit-Bull of American Television turned towards the child and answered her in a soft voice that betrayed him, "How are you feeling, my lamb?"

"Good. I feel better," Melody smiled, showing dimples in her newly apple-hued cheeks. "The Doctor made me all better, Daddy. And I had a dream when I went to sleep."

Randal blinked. He whispered, "*You did?* Tell Daddy all about it, Sweetheart." Randal wiped grateful tears from his eyes and sat down on the couch beside his little daughter.

"Well . . . there was this long, long train and it went off the track and a lot of people were hurt and it made them cry, and I dreamed about a big fire." Her words came in a rush as if she were in a race against time to fill her father in on events only she'd seen. "People jumped from the windows of a very tall building. They were scared, Daddy— *they were scared!* Then I dreamed about a big, big boat. It was away out in the ocean, and a lot of people were on it. And it sank!" She buried her face in her tiny hands. "The people . . . the people jumped in the water and were crying! It was like I was watching *telebision*, Daddy. Like I was watching the news." The little red-haired child reached up with both hands, touching her father's bearded cheeks. Melody's usual routine was to giggle while taking her father's face in her hands, insisting he was turning into a bear. But now, she grew strangely quiet, and the elf-smile dropped from her tiny mouth. Sounding confused by her own words, the child murmured, "*Why* are all those people laughing at my Daddy? *Why* won't they let you be on telebision any more?" Fast tears ran down the grief-stricken child's cheeks.

Randal turned to the couple sitting across the room, a silent question in his pained eyes.

"Carmen, would you please take Melody into the kitchen?" Delgado slowly sat upright in the massive chair. "I believe she is very hungry now, and I would like to have a few words alone with Señor Randal."

Touching her husband's cheek in silent farewell, Carmen

Delgado rose to her feet and crossed the room to the couch. "Melody, would you like something to eat?" Employing a lacy handkerchief, the beautiful woman wiped the tears from her own face and then gently buttoned the little girl's nightgown covering the child's unscarred, flawless, and milky-white chest. "If you'd like, you can talk to my cockatoo, Chi-Chi." Carmen smiled and daubed the tears from Melody's eyes with a corner of her fancy handkerchief. "Chi-Chi likes little girls. You can feed him grapes and he will do tricks for you."

Delgado waited until his wife carried the child out of the room, shutting the door behind herself, before he got down from the chair and crossed the room to the sideboard. "Join me in a drink, Señor Randal." His voice indicated more of a suggestion than a question. "I believe you will need it. I know *I* do. Meeting God's price takes a great deal from a man. The answer to the question you have not yet asked me is . . . yes. Melody is completely healed. And yes, Melody will never be the same. It would seem God has seen fit to bestow upon you a gift of second sight as *His* payment. Rest assured Melody will adjust to it. As you can see, Señor Randal . . . I did."

Delgado reached up to grab the bourbon bottle from the sideboard, and Randal noticed Delgado's white-sleeved jacket's cuff hung nearly over his fingertips.

With a sudden flash of horrible insight, Randal realized he was gravely mistaken with his earlier assumption, when he blithely concluded Carmen Delgado had been married before.

"It seems I find myself at a loss, Señor Randal." Delgado chuckled sardonically, his fingertips brushing the air around the amber bottle. "Would you mind pouring the drinks?"

16

Most Wanted

by

J. Baumgartle

"I'm not sure anyone can really know that," I say, my tone bleakly honest. It has taken our writers' group some time to train me to honesty and I'm practicing what I've learned. I write fiction, and though I no longer consider this a license to falsify human nature, or bend plots, or fight my own characters, I am still in training.

The title they are considering for our next book is subjective, to say the least: "Most Wanted." They are giving me a lot of rope here (joke intended). It remains to be seen whether I can keep from hanging myself.

"You know we have a lot of leeway in developing our ideas," our computer savant gently offers. "Whatever you most want can apply to about anything. . . ."

"I know that, and I appreciate the latitude. It's just that, in my experience, people aren't always capable of making that discrimination. Evaluating your own desires requires objectivity and we're too close to the subject to do that–too much sensory input: feelings, pheromones, mental and spiritual compensations, circumstance and cultural imperative, personality and whim interfere. Which one can we honestly eliminate? Are you referring to perceived wants, or interests, or hidden needs?"

I'm just being myself, and she knows that.

"Your choice."

If there is anything I can't stand, it's freedom to do what I want. Now it is up to me.

I drive home, the confusion of too many choices in my head almost audible. Three months; we have three months to get our stories in. –Our grandbaby is due about that time, too. I'd better get busy.

The first story I write is about losing weight. The main character, Chelz, wishes she were thin again, but doesn't want to get into cute clothes and leave her best friend behind. It's called "Lifestyles."

Whenever I run to town to get more ink cartridges or computer paper, I end up looking through baby clothes and shoes, buying blankets and baby books that can be chewed on.

The next story, though tackled in pieces, is about an old man who wants his hearing back. We sympathize, but observe the teenagers next door who serenade the whole neighborhood with their artless band; hear the mutterings of the living-there daughter who complains about him all the time, the yappings of her little dog, Foozu, and the sirens that constantly go by their house.

Week follows week. I try to space errands around possible phone calls, in case my daughter needs me. Lots of times, I rush to answer the phone and get a political recording, or the Fraternal Order of Police with a capital-letter request for funds. Sometimes the call is a satisfactory service follow-up, and once in a while, a real person.

My latest story (for some reason) centers around the birth of a baby, and all the expectations parents and grandparents have for it to embody, and to realize in the future. The poor little spirit is encumbered with university choices, taste in music and religious preference before it is even born, and all it wants to do is to live. This is my best story. I'll turn it in at the next meeting.

There is a full moon, tonight. I am restless, and wander the dark house, unable to focus on a book.

A little after three, the phone rings, and my daughter says she is on her way to the hospital. It's a three hour drive for us, and the third child for her. We hurry.

When we arrive, they have decided to do a cesarean. No one has time to talk to us. In the eternity of contained agitation, we force even our thoughts to be positive, review God's imperatives for Him so He knows what to do, take stock, ache inside with wanting this baby to be all right—our adult baby, too— recount other births that turned out well, before they come out to tell us everything is okay, mother and baby are doing fine. All our troubles fall away and there is ecstasy nobody has ever experienced before as we go in to meet our new grandchild, and congratulate our children.

There is a lot to do, now. The other grandchildren need us. Their house has been neglected for the last month and could use cleaning, the laundry needs to be caught up, food made ahead in preparation for the homecoming. Recuperation will be more involved

Most Wanted

for our daughter than it has been before.

My husband has to go back to work, but I stay here to help out, flanked by tow-headed little angels who are all interest when their new family member comes home. I love; I love.

In a couple of weeks things settle down.

I finally take my story to the writers' meeting. They pass around copies of our new book. It's the first one I haven't contributed to. It's a good one, though, and I'm proud for them, if not with them. –Another deadline is always in the offing.

I wait and wait; then I pass around my baby-pictures.

The Part of My Brain That Wants to Sell My Writing

by
Marian Allen

The part of my brain that wants to sell my writing
is the part I want to destroy.
If I could send a bullet
into that pocket, bulge, or fold,
the pistol would be
in my mouth
now.
If I could stick a straw
up my nostril
and inhale a drug
that would fry
just that piece of my mind,
I would be snorting
even as I write.
Come, Science! Come
with your lasers
your scalpels
your manuscript
uptake inhibitors!
Smother, strangle,
mangle, excise, alter,
blast or burn
the urge
to sell.

Unexpected Favors
by
Ardis Moonlight

Evan watched the frown lines above his mother's eyebrows and sighed.

"Are you sure you don't want me to call Martha's mother and let her know you're on your way?"

He rolled his eyes.

"Well . . . shall I phone them?"

"No! I already told Martha I'd be there between 2 and 2:30." He glanced at his watch. "It's 1:30. I'll be fine. Stop worrying."

"It's just that—"

"Mr. Brickman showed me the trail. It's not far. I'll call you when I get there, okay?"

More frown lines, then she nodded. "Love you."

"Yeah, Mom."

He dashed down the long backyard, not looking back.

When he got to the gravel road, he followed it until he reached a white marker. This was where the deer trail started that would lead him to Sassy Creek. He and Mr. Brickman had gone down part of it.

When Evan reached the downed sycamore blocking the path, he stopped. This was as far as they had come. Brickman had said the path went on downhill to the creek. He had told Evan to squint his eyes and look for the trail. "An animal walks a narrow path. If you soften your eyes, you can see where the grasses turn outward, pushed aside. It almost creates a silver pathway. You'll see."

Evan guessed squinting was softening your eyes, but hadn't asked.

He liked Mr. Brickman, who was kind of like his dad. Both talked about the wildflowers and grasses his dad was planting on some of the land they owned. His dad wanted to create a small prairie. "It won't be like it once was here, but it'll be a wild place for all kinds of birds plus reptiles." He glanced at Evan.

Evan had wished he hadn't mentioned that. His dad knew he had a big fear of snakes. He felt like he was letting his dad down, feeling that way. He hadn't said anything. But Mr. Brickman had. "Well, Gerry, that's okay, but you don't want copperheads making their homes here."

"Hadn't thought that far ahead, George!"

"If you're lucky, you'll have rat snakes and king snakes come in. They'll keep the copperheads out."

Oh, great, Evan thought. He would definitely avoid his dad's prairie. Rat snakes got really long five, six, sometimes eight feet. He had read a lot about snakes—always good to know something about what you feared, he believed. He still felt chills run down his back whenever he saw a picture of a snake.

He was abruptly brought back to the present when he sniffed something strong and smelly. Skunk? Evan glanced around, but didn't see anything moving. He raised his left hand to his nose, smelling his dad's cologne. He felt calmer.

Evan thought about leaping on top of the tree, then decided he might catch his clean pants on the broken branches potential jean catchers. Evan also remembered snakes sometimes curled on the other side of a log. Instead, he straddled the white bark, looked carefully where he would be placing his feet, and then slid off on the other side.

The path wasn't as clear here. He stopped and stared into the woods, watching the ground. Ah, there it was. It did seem like a silver trail. A small pile of deer droppings marked the edge of the path. He smiled.

As he walked, Evan heard an occasional bird call. He didn't recognize them, but then he only knew a crow when he heard one. No, that wasn't true, he did know a red-tailed hawk's call, and a bluejay.

It had been tough adapting to the country. His mom and dad—his dad especially—had always wanted to live out of the city. His dad had grown up on a farm in Western Kentucky. His mom, however, had always lived in the city. He and his younger sister Karen had been surprised when she brought chickens home one day. Brickman had given them an old coop. They all enjoyed eating the fresh eggs.

He had hated school for several months the first year. The other kids seemed tougher, not very friendly. But he hadn't been either.

Last winter, he tried out for the track team and made it. Now he had four good friends—Ollie, Louie, Frank, and, of course, Martha.

He could smell that flowery scent she wore—Martha's scent. He smiled.

Martha was why he was taking this path. The highway that ran through Portman County blocked the old lane that once went straight to Edenside Road where Martha lived. If he had walked Rain Splatter Lane, he wouldn't get to her house for another hour. Of course, he could have let his mom drive him, but he would have felt like a real nerd. His mom would have hung around talking to Mrs. Ballard. Jeez!

He heard whistles in the woods and stopped. What was that? Birds?

Evan looked ahead and saw the creek through the foliage. Wow, it was bigger than he thought. Sassy Creek! What a great name!

When he pushed back the leaves on the big bushes almost blocking the path, unseen thorns caught his hands. "Ow!" he cried, startled by the pain.

After leaving the path, Evan raised his hands and watched tiny rivulets of blood marking the thorny encounter. Oh great! He remembered Martha laughing at some corny joke he had told her in algebra class. She had touched his right hand when Mr. Waltz was putting some equation on the board. His heart beat faster thinking about

her. He grinned, wiped his hands on the jeans, and started walking again.

The deer path curved through the grass along the creek. It was pretty here. He sniffed and smelled some faint sweet odor, and wondered what it was. Flowers, he guessed. Or Flower, Bambi's friend. He chuckled.

This was nice. He liked doing this walk.

The path curved to the right, and he heard the swish of traffic. Ahead was the thick, stone tunnel. He could spot the tops of vans and trucks as they rushed over. The woods on either side of the tunnel blocked out the rest of the traffic view and sound.

The tunnel was arched and seemed like an entrance to another world. He could see the sunlight and trees hazily beyond. The arch reminded him of the Roman bridges he had read about in a book about France his mom had.

Following the path that curved inward through a thicket of sharp brambles that grabbed at his hands, jeans, and long-sleeved shirt, Evan cried out, "Ouch! Ow!"

He heard the "AWK!" then saw big gray wings spread and flap ahead of the brambles.

Flustered, Evan tripped, lost his balance and fell forward. Thick branches caught him, so he hung at an angle like an insect in some strange thorny web. The thorns pierced his shirt, face and hands. His feet were still touching the ground. Tears blurred his eyes; he closed them tight, then opened again, seeing better. When he looked at the ground ahead, he shook.

A snake was coiled about three feet from the bush where he hung. Black eyes stared at him. The hairs stood up on his neck and back. Evan closed his eyes. He was going to be bitten and die on this bush, his skeleton found years later by some kid.

Evan tried to calm down. He could hardly swallow. His heart thumped wildly. Maybe he would just die of fright.

Evan didn't want to look again, but he had to.

He squinted. The snake hadn't moved. Its head was nestled in the coils in the patch of sunlight. Evan relaxed a little. It wasn't ready to strike. Then he remembered the descriptions and photos in the reptile book he had. He could see that the snake's pupils were round, not slit, its body had stripes running down the length, and it didn't have a triangular head. So it wasn't poisonous. That helped even more. He stopped shaking.

Evan could smell his own sweat. Phew! He closed his eyes tightly. He didn't know what to do. Then he remembered a conversation with his sister Erin who was 10 years older and lived in Chicago. "Whenever I get stressed, Evan, I have to meditate. It's the only way I can calm down."

He had asked how to do that. The only way he knew to unwind was to run.

"I try to let the thoughts go away, so my mind becomes blank. Anytime something enters, I push it away with an imaginary hand. It clears my mind, and I can think again without worrying."

So Evan tried to let his mind go blank, but the snake kept crawling back, its black eyes staring.

He wished he were already at Martha's. She would put something on his scratches and cuts. He could see her, laughing, touching his chest, his hands. Her short, dark brown hair would glitter in the hazy afternoon. He thought about the funny conversations they had after algebra, and how she would come to the track and run with him after practice.

Evan felt calmer. He had to survive this to see Martha. He slowly opened his eyes and watched the snake's tail disappear in the woods to the right. He listened and heard the soft movement lessen as the snake went further away.

He felt like cheering, but the thorns held him.

Gritting his teeth, Evan braced against the branches and pushed himself back to standing. He gingerly moved away from the thicket and walked slowly into the open area where the huge bird had been. He looked around the grass carefully, just to be sure. The snake was definitely gone.

Evan touched his shirt, which had torn in many places. Thin streaks of blood dotted the blue shirt and his hands. This had been a brand new shirt. He felt his face, which hurt, and looked at the blood on his fingers. He was glad he didn't have a mirror. He probably looked like he had been in a bear fight.

He glanced at the dark patches around his armpits, and stuck his hand under one arm, then the other. Then he sniffed. Well, that deodorant didn't work, and it wasn't fear-proof! He giggled nervously.

Noticing a narrow path to the creek, Evan started down. He could wash off. It happened so quickly, he gasped. His right sneaker slid. He fell, landing hard on the slick grass, then slid the rest of the way to cold, moving water, chest level. He shivered, his hands resting on the sandy bottom.

He felt sore all over, but the water took away some of the pain on his arms, hands and torso. He bent over, and stuck his head in the creek, letting the water push against it. He raised his head up, feeling better. Water dripped down his face. He breathed hard. He had never had anything happen like this before.

Evan needed to get out, but not the way he came. He knew he would slide back.

He slowly pushed himself up, then waded in the water until he found a place closer to the tunnel that was more level and easier to get out of. He thought his wet sneakers might slip again, but they stayed steady.

Reaching the path in the grass, he stopped. He looked for the patches on his shirt. The entire shirt was dark now. That's when he started laughing, and began doing jumping jacks to warm up.

What a story he had to tell Martha!

Deep Blue Secrets
by
T. Lee Harris

Josh Katzen shook his head violently, jostling the cell phone against his ear. "No, Clay. I'm sorry. I just *hate* water."

Dr. Clayton Belderes groaned. Josh could almost see the scarecrow-thin marine archaeologist pacing and ratting up his carroty hair, in search of a convincing argument. "Please, Josh! You're the best archaeological artist and photographer I know. You can make that graphical software jump through hoops like nobody else. Besides, Avi said you were a certified diver. How can you be certified and hate water?"

"Certifiable, more like. Let's just say it was a while back and the decision wasn't mine." Katzen stifled a sigh of his own. Damn Avi Rosenberg, anyway. The good doctor was always angling to get Josh to work with other archaeologists. Usually, it wasn't a problem, but this was another story. There was a world of difference between digging in the dirt and playing in the water. Just when did he mention being certified to dive to Avi, anyway? Damned if he could remember – unlike Rosenberg, who never seemed to forget.

Belderes plunged on. "Oh, don't worry about *that*. The expedition dive master can clear you. Really. You'll just need to check out on safety stuff. We had this grad student last year–"

"Clay!"

"Come on, Josh. How many Phoenician shipwrecks come knocking at your door in a lifetime?"

"NO. There is no wa– Phoenician?"

Ten days later, Katzen stepped from an airport taxi onto the docks of Bodrum, Turkey, and stretched. Joints popped and muscles zinged. Transatlantic flights were a literal pain in the ass, and the short hops afterward were almost as bad. The cabbie chattered in a mixture of Turkish and English as he unloaded the bags from the trunk, then stopped, looked around and asked, "You sure you frien' meet here?"

Over the roar of a launch engine, someone called his name. Katzen grinned, peeled off the agreed upon amount of lira and said,

"Yeah. Pretty sure."

Turning toward the shouts, Josh saw Clayton Belderes leaping onto the docks from a slowing motor launch, waving wildly. Tall and lanky with a shock of carrot-orange hair sticking out from under a disreputable bucket hat, Clay looked like anything but a professor of marine archaeology in spite of the "Property of University of Hawaii" t-shirt he wore.

The cabbie eyed the apparition, then burst out laughing. Climbing into his taxi, he called over his shoulder, "I leave you in good hands. *Iyi günler!*"

Josh waved. "*Size de!*"

Clay came up and pounded Katzen on the shoulder. "Josh! I'm glad you decided to come along on this one. It's gonna be a great season!" He looked after the retreating cab. "I didn't know you spoke Turkish."

"Not much."

"Well, nothing about you could surprise me. It turns out you already know our Dive Master."

Katzen raised an eyebrow. "Yeah?"

Just then, a shout rang out, "Joshua Katzen, you bastard!"

A slim, olive-skinned woman with short, black hair strode toward him across the dock, her fine, dark brows drawn together in a formidable frown. Two deeply tanned young men, one sun-bleached blond and the other as dark as the woman, trailed behind her. Josh blinked, then laughed. "Damn me, it's Roz Eliahu!"

Clayton said, "Allow me to present Dive Master Eliahu."

Breaking into a smile, Roz hugged Katzen, then smacked him playfully. "We worked together for two weeks in the Yucatan and you never once told me you were a diver."

He returned the embrace, noting the look of envy on the boys' faces with amusement. "Well, I can do it, but I don't like it. I sort of hate being wet."

Roz guffawed. "You really *are* a cat, aren't you?"

"It has been alleged."

Clay said, "I hate to break up the reunion, but we have to boogie back to the ship." He indicated the two young men. "These are a couple of my students, Josh, Farley Shelton and Savas Balikçi. I brought them along to help with your equipment." He picked up a camera bag and tripod. "Let's roll, folks!"

The boys scooped up the rest of the bags and trotted after the professor.

Josh reached for his duffle and found Roz watching him. Her softly accented words were almost lost over the sounds of the busy docks. "I'm glad you decided to join us, too. Clay is right, you're the best I've seen with this 3-D stuff."

"I keep hearing that. I almost didn't do it. If it wasn't a Phoenician wreck, I'd still be in Chicago finishing my latest painting."

"And I heard that. Clay went whooping all over the bridge when you agreed." She sobered and jabbed a finger into his chest. "But don't think that gives you carte blanche, mister. You're going to check out on the safety measures like anyone else."

He snapped a salute. "Yes, ma'am!"

"Don't forget I know all about you. You get involved in your work so that time and the earth cease to exist."

He shot her a suspicious look. "And?"

"Don't look so worried. I'm just telling you why *I'm* going to be your dive buddy."

The cocky grin returned in force. "Cool!" He shouldered his duffel and laptop case, then fell in step with her toward the launch.

The craft sliced effortlessly through the water, guided by Eliahu's deft hand on the controls. A veteran of the Israeli navy, the lady was at home on the water. Roz was Sabra, a native-born Israeli, but, because of her American father, possessed dual citizenship, a fact she played to advantage in her post-navy career. Using the skills she'd learned in the service, she set herself up as a Technical Diving expert. Her expertise combined with her ability to travel almost anywhere on the globe put her much in demand.

That was how Josh met her in the Yucatan the year before. Roz had been working with an archaeological team, mapping and investigating cenotes, natural sinkholes that the ancient Mesoamericans believed to be portals to the underworld. His friend, Dr. Avi Rosenberg, was acting as a consultant on the artifacts the ancient people tossed into the wells as sacrifices. Josh had been between projects, and simply along for the ride. It had been a fortuitous ride – for him anyway. The guy he replaced probably wasn't so happy about it. A few days after he and Avi arrived, the original computer jockey had taken a tumble down the steep embankment of a cenote. He hadn't broken anything, but got banged up enough they shipped him home for the duration. Avi was quick to point out that Josh fitted their needs to a T, and he was hired on the spot.

Clay nudged his shoulder and pointed past him to a ship in the distance. Grinning broadly, he shouted over the engine noise, "Welcome to the *Diogenes*, your home for the next few months!"

Belderes was proud of the *Diogenes*, and justifiably so. She was a converted minesweeper like the legendary *Calypso*, the vessel of Clay's childhood hero, Jaques Cousteau. He'd worked long and hard to wrangle the backers and grants necessary to purchase and refit her as a platform for marine archaeology. With the discoveries Belderes was making, she was becoming almost as well-known as her predecessor.

The ship was a beehive of activity. Clayton had told him there would be a total of twenty-two people aboard including Josh. The ship had a small permanent crew of four and the rest were staff and students. There was a picnic air as he boarded. He'd seen the same pre-season excitement on Avi's digs.

A tall, dark young man hailed Clayton and hurried over. His speech was heavily accented like that of Savas. "Dr. Belderes, the captain would like to speak with you when you have a moment."

"Sure thing, Iskender. Tell him, I'll be there ASAP." He turned to Katzen. "Josh. this is Iskender Balikçi. You already met his brother, Savas. The Balikçis are sort of my unofficial students."

Josh shook hands with the boy, who then hurried back to the bridge. Looking after the retreating figure, he asked, "How do you have an unofficial student?"

"They're local boys, sons of a sponge diver. They started off as guides, but show such aptitude for the work, I've been helping them. I'm trying to wrangle exchange student status so they can continue real studies in Honolulu. I think Iskender is more interested than Savas, but it would be a great opportunity for both of them."

"Certainly sounds like it."

Clay waved to someone behind Katzen, then said, "I was going to show you to your cabin and work area, but I need to see the captain so we can get underway. Farley and Savas can show you, if you don't mind."

Farley Shelton came to stand next to him. The sun-bleached blond towered over the artist and seemed to be doing everything in his power to accent this. Josh smiled. Being slightly shorter than average, he'd seen his share of that sort of posturing. He'd also seen the look on Shelton's face when Roz threw her arms around him. Poor kid. He seemed to be unaware that muscle and a toothpaste smile wouldn't attract a woman like Rosalind Eliahu. Give him time, he'd learn. Maybe.

"Grab your stuff, Mr. Katzen. Your workroom isn't far and your bunk is right next to it."

He adjusted his laptop strap and said, "Lay on, McDuff."

Shelton looked puzzled, then brightened. "Oh yeah, that Shakespeare stuff." He picked up the few remaining bags and started for the door, saying, "Savas and I already took most of your things to the workroom. We figured you'd know where they went better than we would."

They went from bright sunlight to the dim lighting of the inside corridor. It took until they stopped at the open door to his new workroom for Katzen's eyes to adjust.

"Your cabin is the door just to the left," said Shelton, pointing a beefy finger in the direction. "We don't usually use keys, but the captain has 'em if you want 'em."

Savas had set the bags out in a neat row and was busy uncoiling cable as Katzen stepped in and looked around. Not a lot of light came through the portholes, but the bulbs in the overheads had been replaced with a higher wattage than the ones in the corridor. It would do nicely.

The dark young man grinned and said, "It is a bit cramped, but as Dr. Belderes is fond of saying, the *Diogenes* is a working ship, not a cruise liner."

"Looks good to me. You guys haven't seen my cubbyhole on the Piedras Rojas dig. Compared to that, this *is* luxury." He placed the laptop case on the central table and unzipped it.

Shelton perked up. "Piedras Rojas? Isn't that the big Moche ceremonial site in Peru that Avi Rosenberg is excavating?"

"That's the one. I've been working with Dr. Rosenberg for

several years now."

"Wow! That's some dig. I saw a show on the History Channel last year about it. All that gold jewelry and stuff? How come I didn't see you on that show? I thought they interviewed all the staff."

Josh shrugged. "I was in Lima, helping the *Museo* catalog the finds from the previous season."

Savas was appalled. "But that is unfair to send you then! I would have refused to go until after the filming."

Shelton agreed. "Damn straight! Me? I wouldn't have missed that for anything."

Katzen smiled slightly and concentrated on positioning his laptop on its stand. What would the kids say to find out that he had *worked* to miss that filming? Likely they'd never understand. He doubted that either of them had any reason to object to their likenesses being broadcast all over the world.

The boys never noticed the lack of response. They were too enraptured by the thought of glittering things.

Shelton said, "Man! That stuff must be worth a fortune. *Two* fortunes. I hope we find some gold stuff on our wreck."

Clayton Belderes stuck his head around the doorframe. "Did someone mention the 'G' word? We don't like that word around here. You can't learn much from it and it causes nothing but trouble."

Josh laughed. Belderes' attitude toward sunken treasure and treasure hunters was well known – and not a good one.

Shelton either didn't know or care about the professor's feeling. He whined, "Awww. Dr. Belderes, what's wrong with a little treasure?"

The teacher's normally affable face looked suddenly strained. "Lots. You two better get out on the main deck. Ms. Eliahu is about to give a lesson on the care and feeding of diving gear. You both need to be there."

As the boys left, Clay closed the door and fished in his pocket. Pulling out a key ring, he dropped it into Josh's hand. "That's to this office, your cabin and the medicine locker."

Josh bounced the set in his hand. "Funny, the guys just said no one used keys on this ship."

"We don't usually, but there have been a few petty thefts recently and with all your equipment...?" He punctuated his words with a shrug.

"Why tempt fate? Besides, on this expedition, you're staff, just like in Piedras Rojas. Staff needs privacy."

Nodding, Josh dropped the keys into the pocket of his khakis and buttoned the flap over them. "Cool. I never object to that."

"I better run. The first few days of the season are always full of the headless chicken routine." He paused with his hand on the doorknob. "Oh yeah. Roz wants you to come find her when you finish setting up. She needs to check you out on safety ASAP. Bottom time is so limited, we want to get started tomorrow morning to make the most of the days we have."

Josh gave the thumbs up and closed the door after his friend. He returned to the laptop and stood with his hand resting on the cool, blue plastic lid. Privacy was definitely to be coveted – and something he'd had in limited supply for too many years. That was supposed to be behind him now. Another name, another life. Certainly, there had been great things in that life, but one fact was inescapable: even if a cage is gilded, it's still a cage.

Sweat trickled from his hairline down his nose. He impatiently wiped it and the unwelcome memories away. Winding his ponytail into a knot at the back of his head, he skewered it with a pencil from the case, muttering, "I need a fan in here."

Early the next day, he was on the seafloor, shooting with the calibrated camera, snapping a pile of amphorae from several angles. He checked the playback. Layer one of the 3-D *should* be complete. Time to capture the actual excavation and get a start on layer two.

He was photographing just ahead of the excavators to get the untouched surface of the wreck into the computer. He'd left the photos of the work in progress to the student assigned as his assistant. As he approached the work site, the girl, May Dennison, was busily snapping shots of two students floating a couple amphorae to the surface. Catching sight of him, she waved and kicked over to the lines to ascend with the other two students.

Finished already? He glanced at his computer. Yikes. Time *was* almost up. Seemed like he just got there. Still, there was time to get a few photos of the cleared area.

After a couple pictures, Roz swam up, her short hair floating like an ebony halo. She tapped her wrist computer and jerked her thumb upward.

He spread his hand. *Five minutes?*

She shook her head and jerked her thumb upward again.

He held up two fingers. *Please?*

Even through the mask, she looked exasperated, but nodded and floated at his side watching her timer. *Two minutes and no more* was loud and clear.

Wasting no time, he finned in for a closer shot of the place the last two jars had been lifted from. He snapped a photo, then stopped and looked closer. Damn. Nitrogen narcosis struck fast, but. . . .

Gently fanning the sediment away revealed the object better. If he hadn't had the rebreather, his mouth would have dropped open. Hurriedly snapping more pictures, he sensed Roz coming up beside him to drag him to the lift lines. He pointed urgently at the object and watched her eyes widen in recognition of the unmistakable rim of a gold kylix emerging from the sand.

She pointed to the surface again.

This time he didn't argue.

Clayton Belderes thumbed the playback button alternately smiling and groaning. "Oh man, I was really hoping we could avoid the shiny stuff."

"Sorry about that, Chief." Katzen grinned and smoothed wet hair out of his face. The ascent with its decompression stops took so long, they hadn't waited to dry off. Instead, they launched up the ladder and across the deck to the command center as soon as they broke the surface.

Clay thumbed back to the first shot. "We were watching on the remote camera and wondered what you'd spotted. We never dreamed– Oh! Look at that. I didn't see that the first time, I bet those are the horns of the handles. Has to be a kylix. Has to be. The rim looks in great shape, huh?"

Roz leaned around to look at the camera's screen. "Word of this will leak out fast."

Belderes ran long, thin fingers through his already untidy hair. "Definitely. We'll have to concentrate excavations on that spot until we're sure we have the last of the damnable stuff."

Katzen frowned. "Will you have to call the police in?"

Belderes' freckled face split in a mischievous grin. "Naaah. I'll just call the Ministry of Culture like a good little boy and let *them* deal with that part." He handed the camera back. "You can kick over the anthill with the best of them, Josh."

Anthill was a good term for what followed. The next morning they awoke in the center of a floating carnival. Watercraft of all shapes and sizes had suddenly materialized as if from nowhere. The mystery of why was solved when Iskender Balikçi brought the morning paper aboard. Belderes took one look at the front page and smacked himself in the forehead. "Republic of Turkey Ministry of Culture *and Tourism.* I keep forgetting the and tourism part."

Katzen looked up from buckling his gear. "Tell me they didn't put it in the paper."

"They sure as hell did."

Josh regarded the growing circus in silence, then said, "Just keep repeating the Rosenberg mantra: It's good for grants."

Belderes' only answer was a faint moan.

Since Iskender was the most experienced diver after himself and Roz, Clayton partnered with the young man to begin excavating the gold. With Josh recording their every move, and Roz and the remote camera looking out for unauthorized divers, they carefully but quickly excavated the first kylix and found another just beside it. There was more, too, but their time was up and they had to head for the lift lines and relinquish the dig to the next team.

When they finally broke surface and handed the wine cups over to the waiting conservators, the people in the flotilla erupted in a round of applause. Clay pasted a smile on his face and waved, then turned away, muttering, "It's good for grants. It's good for grants. . . ."

A third wine cup was buried under a tumble of amphorae. It took the rest of the day to lift the jars off. It was nearly flattened, but the gold still gleamed in the waning daylight eliciting another round of applause from the watchers who had stuck through the monotony of the seemingly endless line of pottery.

Dinner that night became a party. Unlike Belderes, the students thought finding gold was just great. Someone broke out a boombox and a stack of CDs. The mood was infectious and even Clay got onto the floor, dancing with abandon.

Josh sat back and sipped his drink, watching the entertainment. Several bottles of local wine materialized and one was presented to him as Finder of the Shiny Stuff. It was a bit sweeter than he liked, but good. Someone slid onto the bench next to him.

Roz Eliahu reached over and plucked the cup from his hand. Taking a sip, she announced, "Not bad. A shame the cup is plastic. I never like drinking wine from a plastic cup."

He grinned. "Me neither, but the conservators would personally shoot us if we went after the other wine cups."

She laughed. It was a pleasant sound. It didn't last long enough. She suddenly frowned and said, "Uh oh. Storm brewing." She tilted her head toward the door. Katzen followed her gaze and saw Iskender Balıkçi stomp in from the deck. He didn't look happy. A moment later, Savas came in. He didn't look any happier than his brother.

"Those two fight all the time."

"What about?" He reclaimed the cup and took another sip.

"Anything. What color the sky is, I think."

He topped off the wine and offered it to her with a grin. "Sounds like brothers everywhere. Care to dance?"

"I thought you'd never ask."

"Dammit. They must have been hacking at this while we were partying last night." Roz glared at the mangled lock on the conservation lab's door. "It's a wonder we didn't hear it, even over the music."

Josh crouched for a better look. "That's a wreck. What's left will have to be cut off."

Dr. Dora Hardin, the head of the conservation team, fluttered back with Clay in tow. She was wringing her hands. "I came down to open up this morning so we'd be ready for the new objects and . . . oh . . . I hope nothing is missing. Do you think it was the kylikes they were after?"

Clay stepped around her to examine the padlock. "I'm sure of it, Dora. Blast whoever in the Ministry thought a news story was a good idea. We'll have every thief in the Aegean down on us."

"Maybe, but it hasn't happened yet. This is strictly amateur night," Josh said as he straightened from his inspection of the botched job. "Probably a hacksaw then a pry bar when the saw blade broke. Chisel would have worked better – a little."

Clay frowned. "It does look pretty clumsy."

"Clumsy isn't the word for it. If this was a real thief, they'd be in and out and you'd never know until you found the empty place where the cups used to be." He glanced away from the lock and found Roz regarding him with a thoughtful look.

Abruptly, she turned to Clay. "I agree with Josh. I'll be surprised if the would-be thieves got into the lab. Our first priority should be to find a replacement lock and get on with the dive."

Clay glanced at his wristwatch. "Right, as usual, Roz. If we don't get a move on, we'll lose valuable bottom time. Dora, find the captain and start the ball rolling on getting the lock replaced, okay?"

Dr. Hardin set off for the bridge with a look of determination.

Over the next two days, a bowl and four golden plates were excavated and brought up to rest safe with the three wine cups behind a large hardened steel padlock. It should have been business as usual, but the attempted break-in had put everyone on edge. Tension was high and tempers flared. On the evening of day two, the Balikçis had a screaming fight so incoherent and loud that Clayton ordered them to different parts of the ship.

That day seemed interminable and Josh finally retreated to his workshop, grateful for an excuse to close the door. Safe in his oasis of peace, he threw himself into reconstructing the pristine wreck site on the computer and time ceased to exist. When he finally sat back, pleased with the progress, he realized with a jolt the sky outside the portholes was pitch black and the nighttime hush had settled over the *Diogenes*.

Checking the time, he cringed. There wouldn't be much rest before the morning dive, but there was no help for it.

Saving and backing up his work, he closed the laptop and headed for bed. His hand had just brushed the power button when a solid thud reverberated from the deck above. He bolted for the door just as someone called for help.

Topside, Katzen found the first mate and a crewman bending

over Iskender Balikçi by the dim light of an electric lantern. The boy sprawled on the deck, right leg twisted in an unnatural position. Blood glistened on his forehead and the planks around him.

There was no diving that day. The floating gallery was disappointed, but made do with watching the water-ambulance whisk Iskender off to the hospital just as the sun edged over the horizon.

Belderes' normally untidy hair was ravaged to the point it looked like a fright wig. He paced the small hospital room like a nervous cat. Eliahu and Katzen wisely took positions in the corners to avoid being run down.

"But what were you doing on the catwalk at that time of morning?"

The boy in the bed bore little resemblance to the vivacious young man Josh had met the first day on the ship. The stark white bandage wound around Iskender's head accented the sickly yellow of his skin. His voice was faint as he answered, "I go up there a lot when I am upset. To think. I woke early and could not get back to sleep. So I climb up to watch the sea."

"What were you thinking about?" Josh interjected.

Iskender's eyes slid toward him, groggy from the painkillers he'd been given. "I was thinking about my brother and how angry he made me. I was ashamed to have lost my temper before the whole world."

Clay waved the worry away. "Don't sweat it. Everyone was on edge and tempers were near the surface all day. What happened on the catwalk, though? How did you fall?"

The young man frowned. "I'm sorry, Dr. Belderes. I can't remember falling. I remember standing in the wind, enjoying the coolness of it – then I am here. In this bed."

"That's not at all unusual." Roz had been so silent, Josh almost forgot she was there. She continued, "Our minds blot out traumatic events. The important thing is that you weren't hurt worse than you were."

Katzen said, "That's true. It might come back to you, it might not. Best not to worry about it. Just concentrate on getting better."

The boy smiled weakly and gave a thumbs up.

Katzen couldn't sleep. Again. It had nothing to do with bad dreams and less to do with the upsets of the day. It had more to do with heredity. He remembered his father wandering the house all hours in the same way. His father. A man who likely believed him dead – probably hoped so, truth be told. In a way, he was. Suited Josh Katzen fine.

He moved soundlessly over the deck, enjoying the stars. The sky was so clear, it was simply amazing. The spectacle drew him to the railing. He folded his arms across the top and leaned into the cool night breeze that lifted his loosened hair and whipped it around his shoulders. A few moments later, the breeze shifted and blew whispered words to his ears.

"I wish you'd get off that. I had nothing to do with it," he heard.

The response was angry and only just a whisper. "You know why I ask. Such stupidity could ruin everything."

Hmmm. Not good. Be courteous and move away or . . . ah, to hell with courtesy. He glided toward the sounds.

"You're too cautious, Man."

"And you are –"

Katzen never heard what Savas Balikçi was going to accuse Farley Shelton of being, because he broke off as Josh strolled around the winches. "Oh, hi, guys. You having trouble sleeping, too?"

Balikçi looked sulky, but Shelton had bluff and hearty down pat. "Hey, Mr. Katzen. Savas and I were just talking about Iskender's accident. The docs say he's gonna be okay."

"That's what they say," Josh agreed, glancing up at the catwalk. "He was lucky. A fall like that could have killed him outright."

"Yes. It could," Savas growled. Shooting another look at Farley, he said, "If you will excuse me, I must sleep. We will be diving again tomorrow and I am on the first team, since my brother is in hospital."

The dark young man strode away and quickly disappeared inside the superstructure. Katzen commented, "Wow. He's pissed off."

Shelton shrugged. "He's upset about his brother being hurt. Since Iskender's going to be okay, I imagine he'll get over it."

Katzen stared thoughtfully at the closed door until Shelton said, "Dr. Belderes says there's probably only one more piece of treasure down there."

"I wouldn't let Dr. Belderes hear you call it treasure – unless you really *want* to be flayed." He grinned at the taller man. "We won't really know if we have all the items until the amphorae have been cleared and logged, but it looks that way, yeah. One last, large object. Maybe a platter or something."

The younger man stood staring out over the water until Katzen said, "You better head for your cabin, too, if you want to be rested to dive."

"Oh yeah. I'll be okay. I'm on the last team," he replied distractedly. "'Night, Mr. Katzen."

Josh watched the blond head duck into the door and disappear from view. A few minutes later, he took his own advice.

The crowd of watchers had grown with each passing day. They went wild when the last piece, a very large, shallow dish was brought up. A collective groan of disappointment met Belderes' announcement that the gold was cleared and only boring amphorae remained. Most sailed away soon after, but a group of diehards hung on until the last team of the day returned to the surface with only pottery. Clayton watched them go with a sigh of relief.

"Glad that's over," he murmured. Turning to Josh and Roz he said, "The kids can get these pieces in the baths without us. Let's head for the lab and get with Dora for the detail work."

Katzen knew immediately what he meant. Belderes wanted to do the detailed descriptions and photographs of the gold objects. They'd been recorded as they were excavated and brought up, but little else was done. Clay hadn't wanted to take any more time away from the dives than absolutely necessary while golden temptation still sat on the seafloor. With the final piece on-board, they could relax and take their time with it.

"You got it! I'll grab a couple fresh memory sticks and meet you at the lab," he said.

There may have been only nine pieces, but the cumulative effect was awe-inspiring. The three graceful gold kylikes with drawn wire handles were elegant in their simplicity. Two looked as if they had just come from the goldsmith's hands. The third was badly crushed from the weight of the amphorae that had lain on it for centuries.

As beautiful as the three cups were, the shallow dish was the star of the collection. On it, a chariot-borne archer chased an ibex, two wild bulls and a cow as his hounds nipped at the heels of the fleeing animals. It was a masterpiece of embossed gold work and seemed to be a mate to the four plates decorated with leaping animals around the rim.

The last piece was a large bowl with a prancing horse embossed into the bottom. It was the last piece Josh photographed, too. He replayed the images to be sure he'd gotten what they needed, pressed the power button on the camera, and said, "Done."

Belderes snapped his notebook closed. "Good. As of tomorrow morning, they'll be somebody else's problem."

Dr. Hardin looked up from her measurements in surprise. "So soon? I haven't had time to do much to them. Granted, gold doesn't require much stabilization, but. . . ."

"I know, Dora, and I'm sorry. I wouldn't normally take it out of your hands, but look at what's happened in the short time this stuff has been on board. I've arranged with the Ministry to transport it to the Bodrum Museum of Underwater Archaeology first thing in the morning. They can complete whatever conservation is needed there."

"You have a point." Dora sighed as she placed the final piece in the reinforced cabinet. "Still I hate to leave things half-done."

Roz gazed at the items as the cupboard doors closed on them. "Human nature is so perverse that such beauty can provoke such ugliness."

"Beauty be damned," Belderes said as he shut off the overhead lights. "I want that stuff off my ship."

There were lots of nooks and crannies aboard a ship, most of them uncomfortable. The one Josh Katzen waited in was no exception. He shifted slightly in the shadows, black clothing rendering him all but invisible. It was probably going to be a long vigil.

As the night stretched on, he nursed the hope that his watch was in vain. It wasn't. At roughly two a.m., the door at the head of the hall opened and two dark figures slid in. As they neared, Katzen saw they wore wetsuits and dive masks. The larger of the two carried a set of heavy-duty bolt cutters. Josh smiled slightly. They might be amateurs, but they did have a learning curve. Too bad they hadn't applied that brainpower to another endeavor.

He let them get to the door and fit the cutters onto the shackle of the padlock before he moved. As he leapt forward, he was startled to see another dark figure dart out from a spot just beyond the door. His hesitation gave the man with the bolt cutters time to react.

With a grunted curse, the man swung the cutters at Josh. The little artist ducked and came up with a kick aimed at his opponent's throat. The man dodged, but the blow hit him in the shoulder, spinning him into the bulkhead.

Katzen briefly noted the smaller wetsuited man grappling with the other person. He didn't miss a beat this time, but hooked his foot behind his own opponent's knee and thudded him to the floor. The man ooofed and tried to roll to his feet. Josh was faster and delivered a double-fisted blow just behind the ear. The bulky form dropped back to the decking, insensible.

Behind him, he heard a similar oof and thud. Whirling, ready for another battle, he found himself nose-to-nose with Roz Eliahu.

The fight had been fast and noisy. Doors along the corridor slammed back and the overheads flared. Katzen blinked in the sudden brightness as Clayton Belderes hurried forward, wrapping a terry cloth robe around himself.

"Josh! Roz! What the hell. . . ?" His voice trailed off as he saw the two figures on the floor, now groaning and moving.

Roz straightened. "I believe we have your would-be robbers, Clay. Shall we see who they are?"

Without waiting for a response, she wrenched the mask off her adversary revealing a sullen Savas Balikçi.

Clayton looked as if he'd been slapped. "Oh no."

"You want to take your own mask off, Shelton, or do I have to do it?" Katzen prodded the big man with his foot none too gently. "Come on. Playing dead only works for possums."

With a snarl, Farley Shelton sat up, tore off his diving mask and spat a curse at the black-clad artist.

Josh grinned. "If you can't do better than that, we'll have to include lack of originality to your list of offenses."

Much later, as dawn grayed the horizon, Josh Katzen perched on the anchor hoist, avoiding the police circus inside. He'd given his statement – what they wanted of it, anyway. It was a small ship. If they needed him they could find him. He breathed deeply and leaned back on his elbows, looking out over the waves. He was still there when Roz came on deck.

"Hey, you missed the big confessions," she said.

"Yeah? Were there any surprises?"

"Not really. It seems Farley and Savas have been pocketing small items from the digs for quite a while now. The Balikçis have a cousin who sold them on the black market for a hefty sum. The gold was just too much to ignore."

He nodded. "Antiquities are lucrative. More today than they used to be in spite of the new legislations."

Roz sighed. "Maybe because of them. Who knows? Anyway, a few days ago, Iskender caught Savas with an ancient signet ring. They had a row about it."

"The night of the party. I don't imagine Savas would knock his own brother off the catwalk, though. No matter how mad he was. It's just not his style. Farley?"

"Savas seems to think so, but Farley denies it. Unless Iskender suddenly remembers something, we may never know."

"I doubt he saw anything. He was in a real funk and Farley Shelton can be very quiet for a large guy."

She stood, watching the sea. "It's beautiful and peaceful out here."

"Yep. Helluva lot better than that mess in there."

She laughed, paused, then observed lightly, "Those were some pretty good moves you used tonight. Reminded me of the ones I learned in Shayetet 13. Where'd you pick them up?"

Josh stared out at the dawn dancing on the waves. A large fish leapt and splashed into the shimmers, the sound of its impact lost to the wind. Finally he said, "I'd prefer not to go there, Roz."

She stared at him for a long moment, chewing her lip. Suddenly, she laughed and pointed. "Look at that crazy swordfish! He's at it again. Must be showing off for a lady fish."

She leaned back onto her elbows, her shoulder brushing his.

He savored the warmth radiating from her and the play of the morning light on her wind-blown hair. Yeah. There was a lot about this new life that was good, too. Very good.

Deny Me

by

J. Baumgartle

Please,
don't give me what I want,
play keep away.
The shiny ball
passes back and forth
over my head,
(laughter at each end)
forces me to look up.

The Hammock
by
Joanna Foreman

In my musty, mothballed canvas cocoon I sway, suspended between giant black walnut trees, my eyes tightly closed. Dark green leaves rustle high above, a chorus of whippoorwills and woodpeckers, mourning doves and katydids, and crows crying *Caw, Caw, welcome back little girl*. I dangle one leg in the unpolluted May breeze. It is not yet noon.

Inside the dusty kitchen of our summer cottage, my parents fuss and sweat as they eliminate caked mud left behind by spring floods. To my left, I hear Brandywine Creek tumbling over rocks and fallen branches, as she says, "Hurry, hurry, they've discovered our fury." *You'd better run away*, I reprimand Brandywine, as she hastens to hide herself from my mother's wrath.

To my right is our horseshoe court, where tonight I will gaze through the campfire's vapor to a clink, clang, whoosh and a thud, followed by boisterous shouts from aunts and uncles as Mommy pitches a dead ringer, her scoffing challenge to the rest of them to *just go ahead and try* to beat last summer's champion.

Beyond the horseshoe court, milk cows graze among us as though they own the entire farm. Their silent presence is broken only by their snorts and grassy snack-chomping and the occasional *plop-plop* of a cow pie. They are happy cows, and I am a happy girl.

My eyes are still closed, but I have it all memorized from summers past. Behind me sits the Bowman's cottage—a little round trailer with a covered patio where adults drink Millers and play cards way past dark at homemade wooden tables. Inside, it has the odor of aged wood paneling mixed with old people's breath. I hang out over there because of Butch, a boy and a friend, but not a boyfriend, you understand. Butch will eat nothing but peanut butter sandwiches for lunch. Once I offered him a quarter to eat tuna, or bologna, just anything but peanut butter, but he wouldn't. He says it's the only thing that hits that spot in his tummy. Butch Bowman finds the best hiding places in hide-n-seek, and last year he chased me with a little black snake and scared me so badly I made him play Barbie dolls with me for one solid

hour. I listen for the sound of their car; they should be here soon.

Beyond their trailer the creek meanders with a winding trail alongside, scattered with cabanas. Not much farther now and I spy, in my mind, The Root Tree. Tangled inside and out, roots rise a foot above ground from times when high water feasted on rich topsoil then washed it downstream to disgorge it in our cabin. During long family walks, we kids will run ahead to play on the roots until our parents catch up, and finally lose their patience. "Come on—keep up," they will plead, so we'll scramble under the electric fence and spend a sunny afternoon fishing at The Pit, a hole so deep we aren't ever allowed to swim in it. We suspect it goes all the way to China.

I open my eyes now and, sure enough, everything is just as I remember. Straight ahead, our simple, two-room cottage enjoys its one-hundred-year lease on a multi-acre dairy farm. The concrete patio Daddy poured last year shows, fresh and clean, the handprints of my cousins and me. Daddy has pulled our new white '58 Ford station wagon up close behind the cabin, and he removes the block of ice we bought at the icehouse down on the winding blacktop road in Boggstown. By the time I opened the farm-gate entrance into the campground, the ice had already begun to melt, so when I rode in on the open tailgate, my new white shorts got wet, dang it! (I'm allowed to say that.) Daddy puts the frozen chunk in the bottom of the musty old fridge and we're set for Memorial Day weekend.

How does country air smell? Fresh, like our sheets after my mother collects them from the clothesline. Of lilacs and peonies, of mint and rosemary. I fill my lungs with the bouquet of this Indiana camp, and I'm home again. Another Hoosier summer awaits; days of endless fun, and skies so dark at night you can see into the next galaxy.

Daddy says I am his princess when I help him prime the pump with creek water, and we will shout "HIP HIP HOORAY" when the Shelby County Health Department says it's safe to drink from the icy cold well. We trace with our fingers the initials carved by my cousin Marsha and me into the concrete at the base of the pump: "JF MT"

A princess in a canvas throne, I swing the day away while they mop the cabin's gray linoleum floor and scrape its meager furnishings. Only on occasion do I step up on a concrete block to survey adult progress. I peek through the old and dark, foul-smelling screens. I could help them, but I don't. Well, when we first arrived I *did* tote a dead mouse out by his tail and watched him bob up and down as the current took him to his everlasting resting place. But for now the cottage reeks, and I fear I may faint, so in my hammock I remain. Each spring, high water brings the creek bank ever closer to our cottage, leaving a nasty mess inside. Dang, dang, double dang, I say. Always in May, we wonder if we will find our cottage lying upside down in the creek, having succumbed to Brandywine's savagery.

I ask why they exert themselves so. "We're making memories, Sweetie, don't you know?"

Time now for Daddy's beer break, so he joins me in the hammock. He beckons Nopi, my English setter, and her head bobs happily as she paddles across the creek. Daddy waves to Mommy as she cleans the outhouse. (Isn't that the way it usually goes? I shall *not* clean toilets when I grow up.) Nopi scampers up close to us and ferociously shakes off her creek water. Dang it, Nopi!

My Dad and I make plans to fish and squirrel hunt together this summer. I ride my bicycle without training wheels now, so I will attach bushy squirrel tails onto its handlebars, and they will flutter as I traverse Stratford Avenue's sidewalks back home in the city. My girlfriends' eyes will fill with wonder, for they have only *plastic* streamers. I will once again be a surgeon and remove eyeballs from cut-off fish heads. I will serve them to Mommy on a paper plate, and she will scream, "Ooey, Gooey, Accumpooey!" just like last year, and I will laugh my head off. I will dance around the cabin with a new upside-down mop upon which Mommy has drawn a face, and I will have fashioned its thick, white strands of hair into braids, tying their ends with satin yellow ribbons. What shall I name her this year, my imaginary friend?

Mommy stands over us now with a rake in her hand and tries to look insulted. She asks gruffly, "Where have all my helpers gone?" Daddy offers lame excuses and coaxes her to relax. "Hold the phone, Josephine," he says with such a handsome grin. She leans over to kiss him and makes a big show of getting beer on her lips. "Oh yucky," she feigns.

We wait for our guests: grandparents, aunts, uncles, cousins and their dogs. How fine it is for everyone to have someone to play with, even Nopi.

The campfire will be surrounded by stories and family laughter tonight as clothes hangers walk around in the dark wearing such fashions as hot dogs and marshmallows. Crickets will chirp background music and fireflies will beg to be collected. When we finally slide into our feather beds made up with flower-fragranced linens, I'll nuzzle my head onto an old goose-down pillow covered with blue-striped ticking, and share my little bed with a cousin more often than not, but some grown-ups will sleep in station wagons or in back seats of Chevys, for the cabin is tiny, but I never hear a complaint from anyone. Mommy will reach up to pull the chain from the overhead light.

Daddy will say, "Who darkied da hole?"

At sunrise Daddy will rattle metal spoons against metal pans and holler, REVEILLE, our bugle call, just like when he was in the Navy during WWII on the *USS Cliffrose*. No one was allowed to sleep in then, so why should now be any different? But we don't *want* to sleep our days away, because there is too much fun to be had.

Ducks quack when we feed them dried bread crusts, as we hike across the shallow end of the creek to the big, white farmhouse. The old red barn is a sacred cathedral with sweet smells of fresh cream mixed with new hay. We pay our rent to the farmer who invites us to visit anytime, and be sure to pick his field corn and search the woods for the rare morel mushrooms. Such delicacies! Mommy sautés them with butter in Grandmother's cast iron skillet, and we close our eyes to savor each bite.

Soon black and yellow bumblebees will bore holes and build nests under the eaves, and lie in wait for weekends when little cousins will become their horrified moving targets. They never really sting us, but we believe they will because they buzz so loudly. We will push each other on the tire swing hung on neighbor Tom Riley's sycamore, and listen to our Indy 500 broadcast in stereo sounds from AM radios all over the campground. We will leap off the tree that, years ago, fell perfectly across the deep end of the creek, and we will splash and swim and shudder when we remember that one day, long ago, a boy drowned here. We will run around barefoot and pull leeches off each other without a second thought. Just who can skip flat stones the farthest across the creek? We will climb the tallest trees, collect paw paws, and by September will have compiled an enviable variety for next year's school leaf project.

Everyone is welcome at our cottage, and when we watch the little road leading to it, we never know whose car we will spy on Saturday mornings loaded with coolers and casseroles, cakes and cobblers. Steaks and chicken grilled on our campfire, fresh buttered corn wrapped in foil, and no matter what the vast smorgasbord, oftentimes nothing hits that spot in my tummy like a hot dog. Daddy always tells Mommy to see that I get it; Auntie makes a clucking noise with her tongue and says it's a shame the way he spoils me, but I am sure she does not yet fully understand the princess concept. Butch Bowman always gets his peanut butter, and I know for a fact there can be no royal blood in that boy.

Mommy, Daddy and me, all in the hammock now—Daddy's toe tickles Mommy's ear. I'm wedged in the middle, happily suspended in this moment in time.

Is this really true? They tell me it's possible one day, a long time from now, I will have to give up one memory of summer camp, and, if so, which one will it be?

I say I'm okay with that as long as I have a lifetime to make the decision.

I'll Fly Away
by
Marian Allen

It was a September afternoon in 1937, the heart of the Great Depression in the rural Midwest. The sun was still up, but a rain as thin as chicken-bone soup drizzled meanly over Hazelton, Kentucky. Veeda Maitland and her little boy, Willis, dragged into Louden's General Store. Both were shivering and damp; both were smudged with glittering black dust. Veeda was pretty far along in the family way again. Her ankles ached from walking the rough gravel beside the tracks.

The coal train had been through that afternoon, and Veeda and Willis had been coaling. There wasn't a station stop in Hazelton, and the tracks didn't run straight through, but took a sharp turn around a hill in the middle of town and pulled in under a coal tipple. Veeda and Willis would push an old red wheelbarrow down the line and pick up chunks that spilled from the tipple or train. Veeda would sing, usually a church song about having wings, a song about flying to Jesus, although anywhere would do. Every piece of coal Veeda picked up, she thought, *You and me, neither of us goin' nowhere. We'll both burn out right here in Hazelton while the train runs on.*

This afternoon, Mrs. Louden gave Veeda and Willis a handful of soda crackers and a mug of Ovaltine between them, which was about as generous as a store-keeper could afford to be during the Depression.

"You coming along all right?" she asked Veeda.

Veeda put a hand on the bulge under her faded housedress. "Yes'm. Thank y' for asking." She sipped the Ovaltine to make sure it wasn't too hot, then passed the mug to Willis. She did it automatically, the same way she answered Mrs. Louden's question, the same way she did most everything, while her mind ran around its circuit: *Wish I was dead. Skinny, ugly, threadbare, draggle-tailed and hungry. Four years ago, I was a beauty. Now I'm a hag. Be a hag till I die. Wish I was dead. . . .*

"Is it kicking any?"

"Some." *It wants out. It'll get what it wants. Then it'll want it again, but it won't get it, no more than its Mama will. Out. Out.*

A rackety black Ford pulled up, nose in to the porch. Veeda and

54

Mrs. Louden exchanged glances and head-shakes – neither one had seen it before.

A woman about Veeda's age stepped down from the driver's seat and came in, a baby in her arms. She was all made up, wearing a Sunday-go-to-meeting dress, and her hair was freshly done in tight waves. The baby was wrapped up in a brand new blanket, soft-looking as a granny shawl, made out of pink and white squares, with pink and white fringe all around the edges.

"Can you help me?" The woman patted her hair, clearly unused to her finery, clearly proud of it. "We're lost."

The baby whimpered. Pride gave way to worry. She jiggled her arms. The baby cooed, then gave a tentative wail, then whimpered again. The made-up woman wiped a tear from her painted cheek and shushed the baby tenderly. "We been lost for hours. . . ."

"You poor things!" Mrs. Louden poked a few sticks into the cast-iron stove. "You come on in and warm up. Where was you headed?"

"Where you from?" Veeda asked, staring, staring, her eyes as big as Willis', captivated by the woman's freshness, her brightness, remembering how it felt to have enough juice in you to spare for tears.

"We're from Laurel Branch, headed up to Fort Knox. Farrell–that's my husband–he's stationed up there, and we was going up to see him. I reckon I took a wrong turn, somewheres. Lord, I don't know where we fetched up, here!"

Mrs. Louden pulled a creased and faded road map from under the counter and spread it open. "You ain't hardly off kilter at all, honey. Just go over the railroad tracks and turn right. Now, that's a bad road and it's coming on to dark, so take it slow. When you get to the end of it, turn left, and that'll take you right on up into Fort Knox."

The woman smiled again. "Thank you."

"Don't you think nothing of it. What's your name, honey?"

"It's Pearl."

"What's your baby's name?" Veeda asked. Willis sucked on a cracker, amazed at his mother's ability to speak to a stranger.

"Jessica."

"Ain't that a pretty name, though?" Veeda smiled at Willis, pressed against her legs.

Pearl wrapped Jessica's fringed blanket a little tighter. "Better get, while the getting's good."

Mrs. Louden folded her map and put it back under the counter. "Well, Pearl, you be careful, you hear?"

"Yes, ma'am. We thank you."

Veeda watched Pearl tap across the porch and down the steps in her unscuffed shoes. She watched the car reverse and pull away, rattling into the dusk. She sighed and put the empty Ovaltine mug on the counter where the map had been.

The evening passenger train blew its whistle for the turn. The whistle came again, longer. Three short blasts. One long – long, desperately long.

"Lord have mercy!" Mrs. Louden cried, out the door before she finished her prayer.

The screen door's bang, the women's screams, Willis' startled shout – all lost in the wrenching, thumping, endless shriek of metal plowing into metal.

Veeda scooped Willis against her pounding heart and ran after Mrs. Louden, down the tracks and around the bend. *No! No!* Thinking of bright eyes, new dress, waved hair, whole spirit.

Later, they pieced together what must have happened: Pearl had crossed the tracks and turned right but, in the dim and the drizzle, she'd turned onto the second set of tracks, mistaking them for the bad road she'd been warned about. She'd come around the turn head-on to the train.

Mrs. Louden stopped Veeda from getting too close to what was left of Pearl's car. "You don't want to see in there. And you sure don't want Willis to."

Half the town was flocking to the site, women in faded dresses and men tucking their after-hours shirt-tails back in, both shooing the barefoot children away. Veeda put Willis down. "Run back up to Miz Louden's porch with the other young'ns, honey. Mama'll be back shortly."

She had spotted what the others had missed, and it was something else she didn't want Willis to see.

The baby – Jessica – had been thrown clear of the car and into a bush. She blinked up through the misty rain and the glare of the train's lights.

You can't get stuck here, honey, your momma's waitin' for you.

Veeda reached into the bush and lifted Jessica clear, cradling her above her own swollen belly. "Doc! Doc Jackson! This baby's alive!"

The doctor turned from the wreck. As his outstretched hands touched Jessica, Veeda felt the little spirit flutter and depart. Doc Jackson took the body. Veeda's tears fell into her empty arms. Tears of joy. *She's gone. She's free.*

Doc Jackson called the state troopers on the general store's telephone and they came, reporters in their wake, to take charge. Mrs. Louden told what little she knew about the victims. Somebody telegraphed Laurel Branch and Fort Knox, a gang of men cleared the tracks, and the train carried its passengers along.

Pearl and Jessica were cleaned up and sent back to Laurel Branch in the undertaker's van. Veeda came to see them off.

Three months later, a girl was born to Zack and Veeda Maitland.

"We'll name her Hazel," Zack said.

"I got a different name for her," said Veeda.

It took him a minute to realize he'd been contradicted for the first time in their marriage. "Hazel, after my momma," he reminded her. "I always said we'd name the first girl after her."

"I already talked to your momma. She said the second girl would do. This baby's got her own name. Your momma understands."

"What's this baby's name, then?"

"Jessica Pearl. This baby's name is Jessica Pearl."

Veeda smiled down at the infant in her arms, then raised the smile to Zack. It was a mother's smile, as hard and sharp and handy as a hatchet.

"Well, if it's okay with Momma," he said, "Jessica Pearl it is."

Veeda cradled her child, beaming a pride as fierce as prophecy. "You watch this girl," she told Zack and the hovering midwife. "This girl is going places."

Lost

by
Ardis Moonlight

The photographs are fading,
      their corners held with black triangles, once secure,
    images of people in places
        my parents knew,
    worn through and through in scrapbooks,
      page fragments releasing.

The album we wanted went missing
    in the Alzheimer's unit
      with the blouses, the shoes,
      the dresses, the skirts, the shirts,
      the sweaters, the slacks, the jewelry,
      the minds.
    They removed things from each other's rooms,
      as girls borrowing gowns and heels
      in college dorms,
      without permission, without thinking,
      theirs to wear until someone took it, too.

*She was a child with bangs, a wide-brimmed sailor's hat with
matching cape,
high-buttoned shoes, holding her Poppa's hand, he with bowler,
vested suit, thick mustache, both serious beside the new black car
with running board.*

We wanted to hoard the pictures of her childhood
    for nieces, grandnephews and ourselves,
    but the album went before she did,
    lost by lost girls and boys.
And what we'll never retrieve could not be restored
    with photographs.

Luxury
by
J. Baumgartle

A huge butterfly
hovers over the tiny blossom,
wings absorbed
in timed heaves,
either leaving a secret
or taking one away.
A giggle flies past,
echo of blue jeans
and tee shirt,
speed suddenly
an obstacle;
surprise in my arms,
deciding it's not hurt.
In all this,
my mind
is never far away
from that little flower.

Small Comforts

by
Glenda Mills

When Dad was diagnosed with cancer at the relatively young age of 68, the initial reaction was sadness and fear. He had metastatic melanoma, and all of us understood the prognosis. My grandfather had died of lung cancer back in the late 1960's, a time when treatment options were slim. When the mole on Dad's back began to grow, so did his fear. He couldn't face going through what he'd watched his dad endure, so he put off going to the doctor. With each surgery, each scan, each treatment, we knew that eliminating a tumor in one place was only a temporary fix, a way to forestall the inevitable, but when time is working against you, stalling is the best you can do.

For four years, he remained outwardly healthy and strong. He was as active as he had always been, and just as opinionated and stubborn, as well. Dad was still Dad, and there seemed to be no reason for immediate concern.

It wasn't until the last couple months of his life that the reality of Dad's illness came crashing down on all of us. The decline in his health was rapid and dramatic. Suddenly, the man who was never at a loss for words couldn't put a coherent sentence together. The grandfather who never missed a soccer game didn't have the strength to walk from the car to the field. The determined soul who had vowed to fight battle after battle for as long as he could enjoy life had to accept the fact that he was going to lose the war. And those of us who loved him had to begin the process of letting go.

For Dad, the process of saying goodbye included making sure he told us things he was afraid he'd never said before or hadn't said often enough. It was important to him, but it really wasn't necessary. I grew up in a home where love was lived, not spoken. Dad told me he loved me by providing for me, supporting me, and interweaving his life with mine. We didn't often hug or kiss or share physical contact, but we played chess on nights when Mom worked third shift at the state hospital. We constructed buildings and landscapes together for Dad's model railroad. We played tennis and watched football games on Sunday afternoons. We spent six years riding back and forth to school together every day, often without speaking. My father taught industrial arts at the junior/senior high school I attended. In the mornings, our silence stemmed from the fact that neither one of us could utter intelligent sentences before noon. However, a lot of our quiet time came from an unspoken understanding that being in each other's company was enough. The only letter Dad ever wrote me was actually a note he sent shortly after I left home for college. In it, he mentioned how lonely the drives to school were without me and how much he missed our time together.

Mom and Dad lived out their love in the same way. I rarely saw them show any physical affection to each other. They didn't routinely say, "I love you." In fact, especially on family vacations, they said a lot of things, most of which did not translate into caring words. They had arguments that resulted in prolonged silence, even short periods of separation, but, when the dust settled, they still had each other. It was a love that survived 45 years of better and worse, sickness and health, poorer more than richer, but with enough money to pay the bills – and usually a little left over.

One of Dad's passions was woodworking, and my home is richly blessed with gifts crafted by his hands. There's the roll top desk he made me when I was twelve and the grandfather clock that was given as a wedding present. He made my husband a display case for his John Wayne figurines that looks like the outside of a saloon. For my daughter's first dollhouse he built an exact scale replica of our house. My youngest received a motorcycle on rockers complete with a taillight and personalized license plate. For Christmas one year he crafted a beautiful portrait of Christ using different types of woods with varying hues to create an image as lifelike as any painting or drawing. As it happened, that same Christmas was the last one I celebrated with my father.

The final few weeks of Dad's life were spent in a nursing home. Mom had promised him she wouldn't put him in one, but he had gotten to the point where she simply couldn't meet his needs at home. She was at his side day and night for the entire time he was there, feeding him ice chips, swabbing his mouth with wet sponges, talking to him, holding his hand when he was restless or upset, and making sure he was being given his medications so he wasn't in pain. The day Dad

died, Mom had left him long enough to go home and feed her cats. I was there, sitting with him, waiting for her to return. His breathing was so labored that each breath seemed like his last. I remember telling Dad he couldn't die until Mom got back. I knew she would want to be with him.

While Dad and I were alone in his room, I caressed his hands and face and told him how much I was going to miss him. I assured him we would all be okay, and that my sister and I would take care of Mom. Dad had not physically passed on, but the man I'd known for forty years was no longer present within the body I held. To watch him endure the weakness of his condition was torture to my soul, and so I prayed for God to take him home, knowing that when He answered my prayers, Dad would find peace and I would be left with an emptiness that no one else will ever fill. The same love that desperately wanted to keep him close knew it was time to let him go.

As it turned out, Mom and I were both with him when he passed away. We were sitting beside his bed, eating his lunch and talking about the state of the world in general. His final breath was the same as all the others he'd taken that day. When we realized the pause had been too long, Mom and I went to him, called his name, held his hands and discovered we were not as prepared to lose him as we thought we were.

When Dad was first diagnosed, he said he wasn't going to seek treatment. He was just going to let the cancer take him. But he did fight, and for four years he enjoyed life. He suffered for only a short time and died quietly and peacefully, surrounded by people who loved him. He had the chance to say his goodbyes and so did we. He was laid to rest beside his father, with an oak tree, his favorite kind, to shade him. I will never forget the sadness that was a part of our lives during Dad's illness, but I will also never forget the blessings that were there as well – small comforts for which I am truly thankful.

Whitepink Promise
by
Bonnie L. Abraham

Crans plucked the Whitepink bud from its vine, carefully leaving a stem just the length of his mother's favorite vase. She would be pleased by the token of his affection and Crans very much wished to please her.

It wasn't that his parents didn't love him. He knew they did. But he also knew that in some circles a child with no magical abilities was considered a disgrace to his magical parents. His youngest brother, Rist, would leave in the morning for the Academy of Magics – following their sister, Steena, who was already distinguishing herself as a student of great power, and their brother Adeel had just been certified as a mage and offered a treasured teaching position at the academy. Mum had taught at the academy and Da – well, Da is just Defender of the Eastern Border. Then there's me. Not that first glimmer of magic.

Crans remembered the looks of proud approval showered on each of his siblings as they first showed signs of magical power. It was a look he did not ever remember them giving him. He stuck the Whitepink into his buttonhole and trudged homeward. Face it, Crans. They will never look at you that way.

His father had tried, a few times, to encourage him with stories of Hodral, who legend said had not shown signs of magic until he was thirty. Crans had studied everything he could find on Hodral, but eventually had to admit, at least to himself, that he agreed with the best authorities: Hodral had simply hidden his abilities. It had, after all, been in the time following the Great War when magic had been forbidden in High Kingdom.

As he approached, Crans saw his mother, Playit, watching him through the kitchen window. She was chewing her lower lip as she often did when she looked at him and didn't know that he could see. Worrying, thought Crans, because I can't do magic.

He entered the cabin with a smile on his face. Playit was wiping a plate with the vigor of someone who was pretending to dry dishes. He pulled the Whitepink from his buttonhole and gave it to her. "They've bloomed all summer this year."

Playit sniffed the cinnamon fragrance in appreciation. "Thank you. It's beautiful. How were things in town?"

"Olad offered me an apprenticeship in the mill," he answered, getting straight to the point. "It would be a good position. He knows his trade and is fair to his workers."

Playit smiled encouragement. "It's a good trade."

"I would have preferred smithing, but I don't want to work for Eledd. He doesn't feed his apprentices enough."

Playit snorted. Crans was *always* hungry. "There's part of last night's pie in the cold box."

Crans needed no more invitation. Grabbing a fork, he found the leftovers and attacked them even before he sat down at the table.

"Don't spoil your supper," warned Playit as she laced a loop of string onto her fingers and turned toward the fireplace.

Crans put down his fork and, as he often did when his mother worked magic, he copied her movements with his own invisible string. Flames jumped to life and licked hungrily at the wood that had been carefully arranged in the fireplace. He sighed and picked up his fork again. *Nothing.*

Playit turned back to Crans. "Your da and Rist will be home soon and we'll be eating."

"I'll save room."

His mother smacked him playfully on the head, then found her vase and placed the Whitepink bud in the center of the table. "It should be open by morning."

Crans was just washing up his dishes when he saw Rist and his father Willim coming up the path. "They're home," he called to his mother.

Playit came bustling into the kitchen and took the dish Crans was wiping. "I'll finish that. You set the table for me."

"What are we having?"

"Just roast with vegetables. It's what Rist asked for."

Crans nodded. It was what he would have asked for, too. "Glad I left plenty of room."

Willim and Rist arrived in a gust of wind. Dinner was served and consumed amidst talk of school and travel. The evening passed with no more mention of Crans' future plans.

Rist left early the next morning, even before the rest of the family had breakfast. Crans was barely up in time to give his brother a parting hug.

"I'll write you lots of letters," promised Rist, "and tell you everything."

"See you do," said Crans to his brother's departing back.

He felt his father's hand gently squeeze his shoulder. "Let's see what your mum has planned for breakfast."

They found Playit wiping tears. "He's too young to be going off by himself."

"He's older than Steena or Adeel were when they left," said Willim. He gave Crans a knowing smile.

"I cried then, too," said Playit.

"My point exactly," said Willim. "Age has nothing to do with it." He hugged his wife, then rescued the applesauce from the fire.

"Oh! I've let it burn!"

"Only a little scorch," said Willim, as he gave it a stir. "Makes it taste better."

"Crans, hurry and slice the bread for me before the cheese cools." Playit cut into a small wheel of cheese, browned from the fire, and spread the soft golden center onto the slices Crans presented her, then spooned applesauce on top. "Oh. The tea. Willim, will you pour?"

As soon as everyone was eating instead of serving, Playit asked, "Crans, have you told your da about your news?"

"My news? – Oh, about Olad, you mean. He's offered me an apprenticeship at his mill. I haven't said yes, yet, but it would be a good position." He tried to keep his voice even as he watched for some sign from Willim.

"I see," said Willim. "Is that what you would like to do?"

What I would like to do is join the others at the School of Magics. "It would be a good trade, don't you think?"

"Yes," said Willim, with an eagerness that sounded forced. "Good honest trade. Olad would be strict, but fair, and he knows his job. You could do much worse."

"When can we make the arrangements?" asked Crans.

Playit reached out and stroked the Whitepink bud with her finger. "There's no big hurry, is there?"

"No," said Willim. He gave Crans a reassuring smile. "No hurry."

A week passed. The Whitepink remained a tight bud in its vase in the center of the table. No one mentioned the apprenticeship.

"Why hasn't this thing bloomed?" asked Crans that evening. The anger in his voice had nothing to do with the flower.

"It will," said Playit.

"When it's time," said Willim.

"When is it time for us to make the arrangements for my apprenticeship?" asked Crans.

"There's no hurry," said Playit.

"There's no use putting it off," yelled Crans, as he jumped to his feet. "I won't ever do magic. I have to accept it and get on with my life. Don't you understand? Accept it! I can't do magic!"

He didn't remember leaving the cabin. He was halfway to the village by the time the cold night air bit hard enough to break through his anger and frustration. "Should have brought my cape," he grumbled. He stomped on, not knowing exactly where he was going. He had no plans. He just knew he had to *do* something, take some action regarding his future.

There were no lights anywhere in the village when he arrived. A quick search of his pockets produced only lint and a loop of string from the ball his mother kept in the kitchen. He was tired and hungry and cold. "I can't go knocking at Miller Olad's door this time of night. Besides, he said he had to talk to Da before he'll take me on."

He heard footsteps coming his direction at a steady pace and ducked into the narrow alleyway between two buildings. *The guard! He'll send me home!* He pressed his back against the wall and waited.

"What's that, Pudge?" asked a deep voice. "What's the matter, boy?" This was answered by a sharp bark and a growl. "After it, boy!"

Crans ran. He ran around outbuildings and through gardens and over fences, his heart thudding in his chest. The village fell behind him, and still he ran. Trees and vines and thorn bushes reached out and grabbed at him, slowing him. He ran until he fell and couldn't get up again.

His breathing finally quieted and he could hear other sounds around him. But not the sounds he expected. No barking dog, no running guard. An owl hooted. Somewhere to his left, leaves rustled quick and low to the ground – a small animal scampering away. He sat up and wondered where he was. He was still hungry and more tired than ever, but the run had warmed him. He lay back down and fell asleep.

He was awake again long before light. His stomach growled menacingly and he shook with cold. In a wave of homesickness and remorse he remembered watching his mother light last evening's fire. His hands twitched as his muscles remembered the movements. *Useless.* Somewhere he had heard that a person could make fire by rubbing two sticks together. He had always thought it sounded a bit too much like magic to be true, but he was desperate.

Several broken sticks later, aching arms forced him to give up. At least the effort had warmed him enough that he wasn't shaking. And the sun was up. He looked around hopefully for some sort of berry bush. He didn't find one, but he did notice the path he had made. He could find his way back. That thought was quickly followed by the memory of the night before – his anger and frustration, his fear. Back was not where he wanted to go. But what were his choices? His clothes were torn and covered with stains and bits of leaf and twig. His hands were dirty and blistered. He looked like a vagabond. He couldn't exactly present himself somewhere and ask for work.

In the end, he decided to follow his trail. At least he could get out of the forest. He would decide where to go, once he knew where he was. The logic of the thought appealed to him and he repeated it over and over in his head. *You can't decide where to go until you know where you are.*

Finding the edge of the forest took more than half the day. He kept straying onto false paths and backtracking. Thankfully, he found berries and a fruit tree. He gorged himself on the overripe Clingfruit, then filled his pockets for later. In the process, he found the string again and the memory of his mother hit him like a stone. He fell to his knees and wept until he had no more tears. Forcing himself to his feet, he continued his journey. When he came close to the edge of the village, he circled it, heading for the road beyond. He would not go home in disgrace.

Night found him farther away from home than he had ever been.

He was hungry again, and his small supply of Clingfruit was gone. He was looking for a sheltered place to sleep, when he noticed a light ahead. As he drew nearer, he saw that it was a campfire. There were three men warming themselves around it and their voices carried to him in the darkness.

His first impulse was to invite himself into the circle, but something cautioned him. He approached quietly and slipped into the woods, working his way around them, listening all the while to their conversation.

"I tell ya, that little village ahead is prime. Lots of fat merchants with pockets and bank accounts to empty." This was the tall one with his back to the trees. Crans couldn't see his face.

"That's what you said about the last town, remember?" This man's profile reminded Crans of a large pig. His voice even had a grunty, squealy texture.

The third man had a long nose that curled down at the end. It fit his pinched face like an arrowhead on a shaft. "We will amble in tomorrow and take a look for *ourselves*, Kleep, and then decide. Don't draw attention to yourself." He leaned forward, eyeing Kleep. "You give us away this time and I'll skin ya and feed ya your own heart."

Crans saw Kleep stiffen, but the man didn't back down. "I didn't give nobody away. It was Oinks, there." He thumbed dismissively at the pig-faced man.

Crans almost laughed aloud. *Wonder how he got that name?*

"He's the one that had to go and kill the old man," said Kleep.

Now Oinks was on his feet, brandishing a limb from the fire. "You's the one let the old hag escape and find him!"

It was difficult to see what happened in the ensuing battle, but it was the arrowhead-nosed man who was last man standing. Crans was surprised. He was the smallest of the three in every way. Surely the other two could have defeated him easily.

"Now, if you're finished with this nonsense," said Arrowhead, as if nothing unusual had happened, "let's make our plans."

The plans were dull – who would check out what part of town. Crans forced his mind to examine the things he had already seen and what they meant. Had Arrowhead used magic? It was almost more than Crans could believe. He had never really considered his father's title of Defender and what it was he defended against. The wizards his father had told him about were potentially dangerous, but only because they were untrained. He hadn't said some of them were evil. A new kind of coldness seeped into his bones.

When he turned his attention back to the three men, they were readying themselves for sleep. Crans only half watched until Arrowhead stood, held his hands out to either side and began muttering. He turned slowly in place, and the men and their campfire disappeared behind a soft glowing wall. As Crans stood, trying to see where they had gone, the light faded to darkness. There was no sign of the camp.

I have to tell Da. But Da was two days journey away, and that would be too late. Crans pulled the string from his pocket, comforted by the feel of it in his fingers. As he worried with the string, his fingers remembered his mother's lessons. He wove figure after figure, wishing that he had his mother's power. Fire. Gate. Ladder. Bowl. Broom. Spear. Figures came and disappeared, one after another. He didn't remember the names of some of them – didn't even remember ever having seen some of them.

Crans felt as though a fire burned inside him. His fingers worked faster and faster. The forest disappeared and he saw only the glowing string. *Bird.* He lifted his hands as though to release the creature.

He was looking down at the road from a great height. *I'm flying! I'm flying!* He caught a sudden whiff of something rotten and was reminded of the camp below him, hidden in the magic. *I've got to tell Da!* He circled twice, widening until he saw the village, then flew toward home. His arms ached, but he knew he had to keep flying. He had to reach his father.

His eye caught the glow of Whitepinks and he dropped lower. The cabin appeared just ahead out of the dark. He gave one last push toward it. Then everything dimmed and he was falling. *Got to tell Da!* Blackness.

Cinnamon. Crans groaned and opened his eyes. In the dim light, he saw a Whitepink in full bloom on the table. "Da! Where's Da? I have to tell him!"

"Hush," said his mother's voice from somewhere behind his

head. "He's gone to protect the village. It's all right."

"The village? He knew, then?"

"You told us, before you passed out. Thanks to you, he'll be able to save them."

His mother placed a cool, wet cloth on his forehead and smiled down at him. *The magic smile.* "Now, do you want to sleep – or eat?"

"Eat," murmured Crans, as his eyes closed.

When he woke, sun was pouring over him. He shut his eyes against it. "Where's Da? I've got to tell him!"

Something blocked the sun from his eyes and he opened them. Willim stood over him, beaming almost as brightly as the sun.

"He doesn't remember," said his mother.

"It's all right, son," said Willim. "Thanks to you, the village is safe and your Arrowhead and his gang are confined." He held out a bowl, with steam rising from it. "Now, I suggest you have some of your mum's stew before you try any *more* flying."

Instructions for Seagull (Bird) string figure

by

Bonnie Abraham

Terminology:

Basic position: hands held fingers up, palms facing each other. When holding a loop of string, the hands should be far enough apart to hold the string snugly.

Portions of the loop of string are named according to the finger around which it is looped and its proximity to the body.

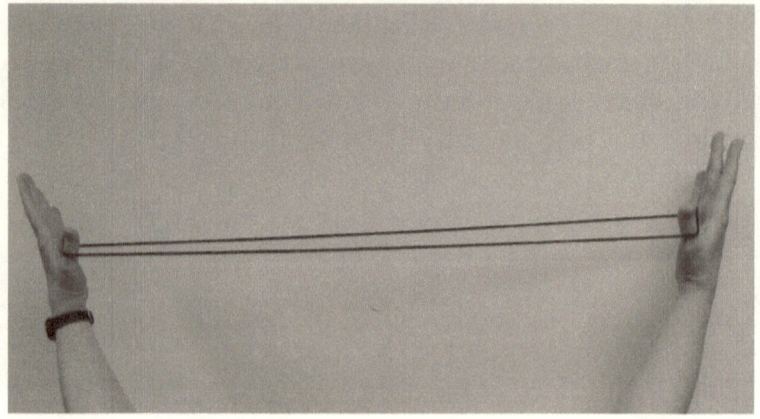

1. Hold hands in basic position with a loop of string on the thumbs. You now have a near thumb string (closest to you) and a far thumb string.
2. With the pinky fingers, reach under and pick up the far thumb string on the back of the pinky fingers. You now have a near thumb string, a far pinky string and right and left palmer strings (the strings running across the palms of your hands).
3. With the right index finger, go across and pick up the left palmer string from below with the back of the finger, and carry it back

as the hand returns to the basic position. With the left index finger, go between the near and far index strings and pick up the right palmer string.

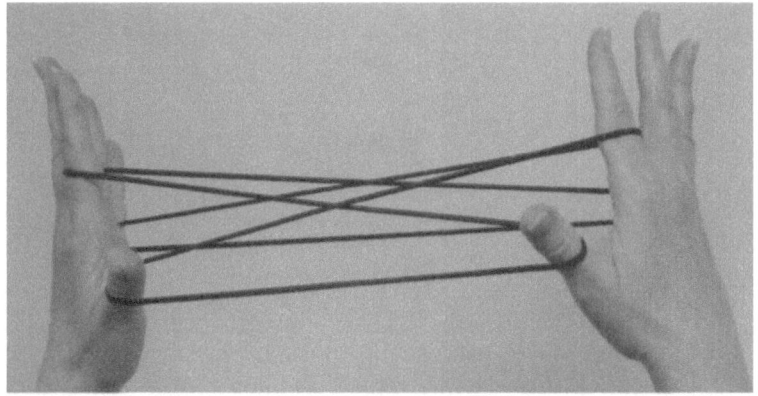

(You now have Opening A. Many figures start with this opening and often, written instructions with say, begin with Opening A, omitting all the instructions so far.)

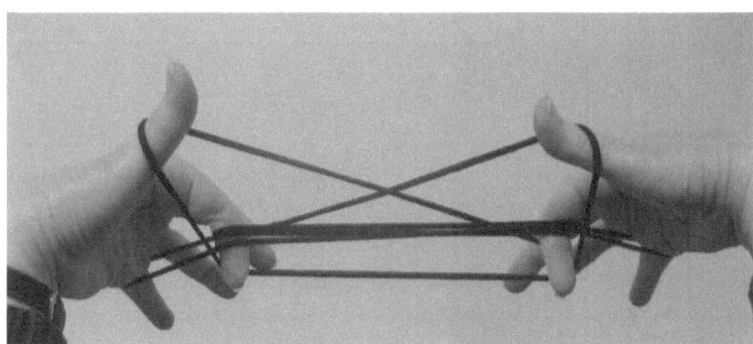

4. From now on, both hands will act in unison. Once you learn the figure, each of the following steps will flow into the next, almost like one continuous motion.

5. Index fingers go outward, over all the strings and curl back under them to go over the near thumb string and hook it back, removing it from the thumbs, as hands return to basic position.

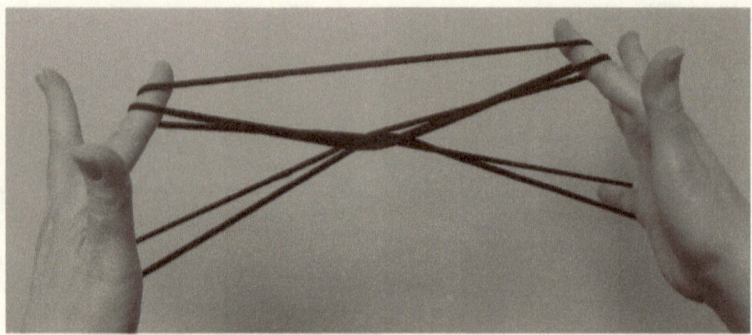

(You now have only one string that isn't crossing the others, the near upper index string. The near lower index string is divided into right and left.)

6. Thumbs hook down near lower index strings.

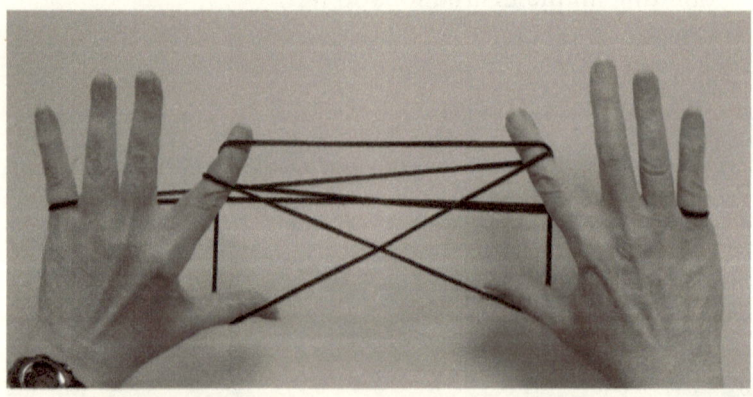

Palms turn outward and thumbs pick up far pinky string (it should be the straight one on the bottom) on back of thumbs, drawing it back through index loop as hand return to basic position.

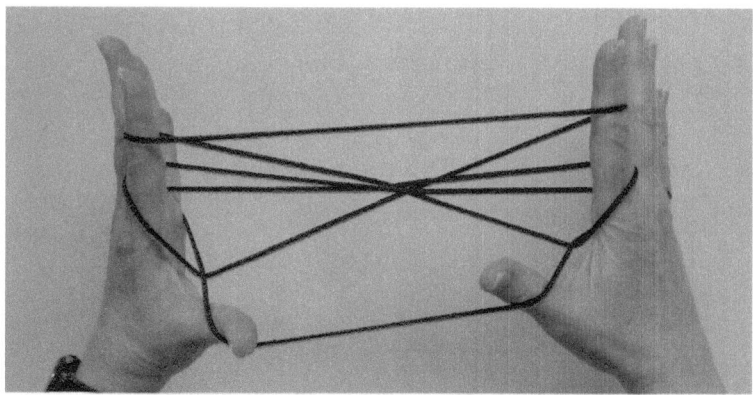

(Note: I did not rename the index strings because the thumbs don't keep them. The thumbs just hold them down in order to bring the pinky string over them. The same applies in the next step.)

7. Thumbs hook down near upper index string, letting thumb loop slide off. Still holding down index string with thumbs, turn hands so fingers point away. You should see the near pinky strings like the bottom of an X in the box made by the thumbs.

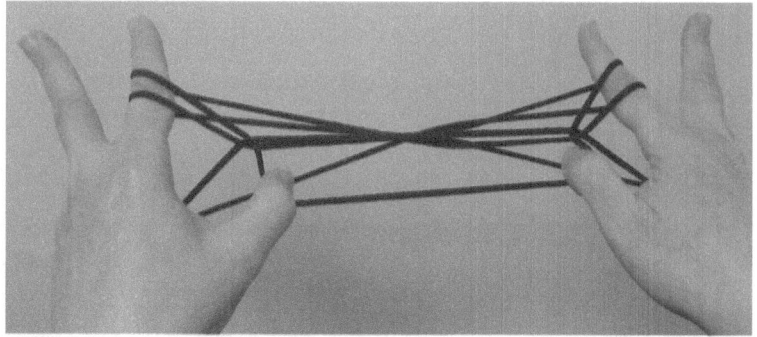

Hook the pinky strings with the backs of the thumbs and draw them back through the index string, letting the index string slide off thumbs.

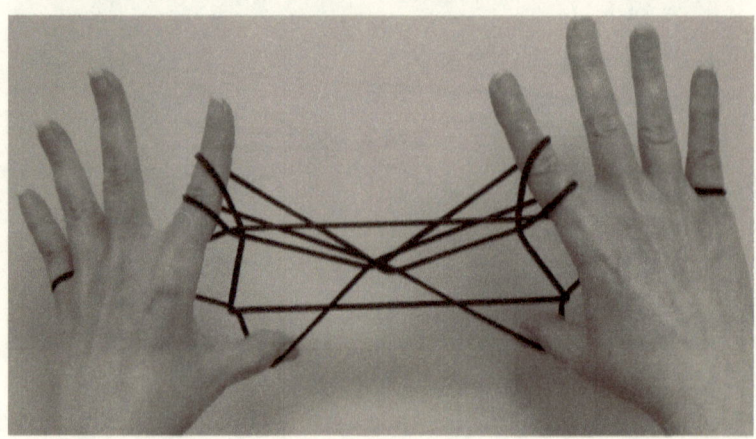

8. Turn hands palms out. There should be a straight string running behind the thumb loops.

   Catch the string on the backs of the thumbs and draw it back through the thumb loops, letting the old thumb loops go. Return the hands to basic position and release index loops. Extend the figure.

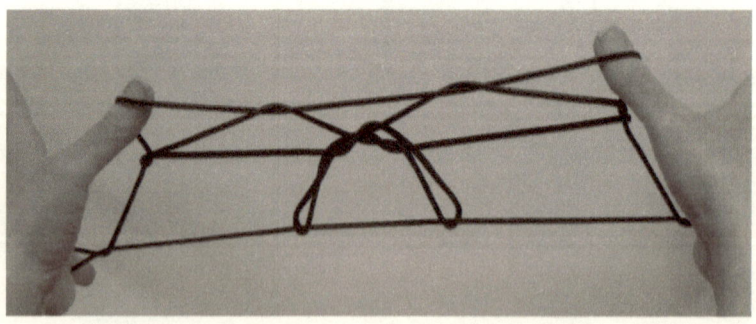

Coiled Persistence

by
Ardis Moonlight

What a patient predator,
       waiting under low planked docks or by
A lily pad, scaly head feeling jawbone vibrations;
       brown-striped
Tributary pushing warm lake shallows, creating
Effortless serpentine shapes.   Limbless, elongated
Reptile homing, like a missile, for a meal.

Sinuously navigating cattail stalks,
       narrow tongue collecting
Nuances of vegetation, small fishes and amphibians.
Alert round pupils notice any movements.
Kin to alligators and turtles, the frog gulper
Enters reedy labyrinths— a whip flexed, waiting.

Goodbye, Baby Boy

by
Joanna Foreman

I check my rear-view mirror for the boy's image. Two hundred miles down, three hundred more to go. I see him now in his little black coupe. Is he smiling at me? No, he's just smiling, I think. We travel caravan-style, both vehicles loaded to the hilt with the past eighteen years and two days of his life—guitar and sheet music; boxes of books and unfinished manuscripts; new bed linens for the dorm, and electronics like CDs, video games and his PC.

His girlfriend insists he take her pillow. She wants to be in his thoughts when he drifts off to sleep. Dream on, girl—he's forgotten you already. This male is on the scent of a *new* life. His older brothers easily managed to do the same in our hometown, but does he? Oh, no, not Jordan. He makes a huge production out of it, moving so far away to a renowned college town.

He was elated when accepted to the university. The suffering from his father's death he hoards within his fingers—writing is therapeutic. He will be a famous author.

Dubuque Street—We pull up in front of the Mayflower Residence Hall for our turn in the unloading zone. Jordan carries his computer, and I grab a suitcase. Two puny elevators groan and take their sweet time. I want to be useful, but he won't even let me put sheets on his twin bed. Okay, fine . . . do it yourself, Mister Smarty. Last trip to the car, he hugs me goodbye right out there on the sidewalk, says he'll call me tomorrow. He waves and he is gone!

How does he do that? Walk away so easily from the woman who brought him into this world. I stand there, dumbfounded. The car waiting behind mine revs its engine. I want to scream, "Can't you see— I am *not* finished here!"

I had planned a mother-and-son parting weekend, and this is only Friday afternoon. How does a mother deal with losing her baby in one eight-hour drive?

The Iowa House Hotel—room 318—reserved for two nights. I sleep fitfully. Saturday breakfast downstairs in the cafeteria. I dine alone at a window-side table—such a grand view of the Iowa River. The aromas of French toast and maple syrup, and the random cling-clang of silverware, comfort me. Students and parents intermingle. I don't dare call Jordan; he doesn't do mornings. How will he make it to his nine o'clock classes?

Outside, it is dark and wet. I read a book and take a nap. I ring him up later. You want to do a late lunch? He doesn't. I am as gloomy as the day, clouds and sprinkles here and there.

I know I need to let him go.

I walk three blocks up the hill into town where I discover The Artisan's Gallery. Well now, Iowa City isn't so bad. I can shop for jewelry and art and visit my son, too. I buy him a signed print by a local artist, Brian Andreas, titled *English Major*:

> "*I told him I was an English Major and he said, 'Too bad for you, this is America.'*"

And one for myself, *Enough Time*:

> "*Everything changed the day she found out there was exactly enough time for the important things in her life.*"

Back at my room, I think of my son's father. What would this day be like if he were still here? Fifty is much too young to die. I am the sole parent for three years now and closer to my sons because of it. *Have I been good enough for them?* That question runs around in circles, and I can't focus on anything else. My youngest is still at home—oh, I forgot—not anymore. He's across town and definitely not thinking about his mother. Tomorrow I will go home, but he is there already.

Leaving him here is tough. For me.

I close the drapes in my hotel room. They don't quite meet; they never do. I prefer basic beige to gray sky. I stack pillows on my bed, stretch out and read Anna Quindlen's book, *One True Thing*. Wouldn't you know—it's all about motherhood. Is there a message here for me?

Ellen's mother is dying of cancer. From her deathbed she runs her household. I think of my mother's cancer and her death. How do I measure up to her as a parent? Motherhood was my sole career. What am I to do now that there is no one left to nurture?

A cloud opens to expose a single beam of light that filters fine and shiny dust particles across the room onto the bed. Abruptly, my brain chemistry rearranges. The universe has answered my question. *I AM GOOD ENOUGH.* The ray of light disappears as quickly as it emerged, and the sky is overcast for the remainder of the day, and yet. . . .

Everything changed the day she found out there was exactly enough time for the important things in her life.

I write a letter to my son on the back of his English Major print. "I'm happy for your new life, and I will go home now and have one of my own. I fear I haven't prepared you to live so far away, so call me when you do laundry. If you'd rather your white shirts be pink, just wash them with your reds." (Just in case he doesn't call me . . . and he won't.) "And one important thing to remember: Always, always, always ask questions.
Love, Mom."

I deliver his print. He doesn't get it, the English Major thing. He will . . . someday. He springs for dinner at the Brown Bottle, an Italian Restaurant downtown. With an authoritative voice, he orders Chianti. I cringe—surely the waitress will card him—but she doesn't. She returns to display the bottle on her forearm. He nods, she pours, and he swirls and sips. He nods once more, like he's an expert at the process. I worry: Is this a sign of things to come in this tawdry, decadent college town?

What kind of a mother would leave her baby here alone?

The next day I begin my journey home. Before the sun comes up, I pass the Mayflower on my way to Interstate-80 East. With a lump in my throat, I say a silent goodbye to my curly-haired little boy, and I cry until I cross the Mississippi River.

I have let him go, I think. We're both going to be just fine.

Danny's Pictures
by
Glenda Mills

Nothing much ever happened in Chandler, and that suited Jack just fine. He'd done his serious sheriffing back when his eyesight was keener, his hands steadier. Nowadays, he drank less whiskey, prayed more often, and watched sunsets from his rocking chair on the front porch of the town jail. He'd never raised a family. When he was younger, he'd been too wild to tame. Now, he was just too tired.

"You headed over for lunch soon?"

Jack looked away from the wall where he'd been nailing up the new wanted posters that had come in on the morning stage.

"I reckon it's about that time," he said, checking his pocket watch as much out of habit as anything.

Billy, Chandler's newest and only deputy, nodded. "I'm going over to Miss Emma's. She's serving chicken and dumplings."

Jack looked behind him at the two empty cells. "Seeing as how there's no one here to worry with, I think I'll have some dumplings, too. Okay if I tag along?"

Billy nodded again, and the two men left.

Billy, whose Christian name was William Knott, was a good deputy who took his job seriously, no easy feat in a backwoods town where the most serious crime in years had been a case of domestic horse theft. Mrs. Barker had walked to Chandler one evening looking for Mr. Barker and found his horse tied up at the saloon. In a blaze of righteous anger, she mounted the animal and rode it out of town, leaving her very drunk husband to stumble home hours later, but not before he'd reported the thievery.

When they got to Miss Emma's boarding house, her son, Daniel, was sitting on the porch. Without a word, he handed Jack an envelope.

"Hi, Danny. Did you draw me another picture?"

The boy smiled at the sheriff, then waved to Billy, who waved back.

"Well, partner, I'll be sure to look this over as soon as me and Deputy Knott have some of your mama's apple pie. How about that?"

Danny's smile broadened. Jack folded the envelope and stuck it in his back pocket. "You stay out of trouble, young man, or I'll send Deputy Billy out here after you." He used his most serious sheriff voice, but the boy was unruffled. Still grinning, he waved to Billy again, then to Jack, and turned away to watch a bird on a branch above the porch.

"So, are you going to open Danny's envelope?" The two lawmen were surrounded by empty bowls, once full of chicken and dumplings, but now wiped clean by thick slices of Emma's sourdough bread. Their coffee cups and stomachs were both full, and the apple pie was on its way.

"I'll wait. He draws real good considering he's only eight. Last week, he gave me a picture of old man Livers mare, the one that died over the weekend while birthing her foal."

"Does he ever say anything? I've never heard him utter a word, just smiles and waves."

"Danny can't talk, or at least he never has."

The two men saw Emma coming with their pie and waited until she was out of ear shot to continue their conversation.

"Back when Danny was born, he was having a hard time breathing. He was getting worse, so Tom went to get the doctor. Tom was Emma's husband. Well, anyway, while Tom was gone, Danny quit breathing all together. Emma said he went cold and turned blue. He was dead, and she just held him and cried and cried."

Billy was hanging on every word, a perfect time for Jack to stop talking and take a big bite of pie.

"Wait just a doggone minute. That boy out there on the porch may be quiet, but he ain't dead. I think you're fooling me."

"I'm telling you the truth, I swear. The doctor got there a few minutes later. He said it was a miracle, what happened next. Danny all of a sudden opened his eyes and took a lung full of air, then another and another. He's never been quite right, though. I figure it goes back to all that trouble he had as a baby."

"Where's his pa?" Billy hadn't had one bite of his pie.

"Tom was knocked off his horse on the way back from getting the doctor. They found his body the next morning. Emma sold the farm, moved to town, and opened the boarding house."

Jack sat in his rocking chair on the front porch of the jail, waiting for sunset. Billy was out making the rounds. From behind the jail, Jack heard a rider coming in. The man tipped his hat as he rode by, and Jack saw a jagged scar down his right cheek. Chandler didn't get many strangers, especially ones that looked as rough as this guy. The sheriff watched him make his way to the saloon, tie up his horse and go in. Jack figured he'd wait a few minutes, then wander down and have a little chat with the town's most recent visitor. In the meantime, he'd take another look at those wanted posters in his office. When he stood up, Danny's envelope crinkled in his pocket. He pulled it out. "Sheriff Jack" was written in big square letters on the front.

"You finally getting around to opening that?" Billy asked from the doorway, giving Jack a fright that he didn't really need at his age.

The sheriff turned around. "Billy, if I was a few years younger and faster on the draw, you'd be more careful about coming up behind me." Jack tried to sound mad, but Billy's impish smile disarmed him and he smiled back. "I was going to put it on my desk and check the wanted posters. We've got us a stranger in town. He's probably just passing through, but I want to have a little talk with him, just to be sure he's not trouble."

The two men studied the posters carefully. The scarred man's face was not among them.

"Tell you what," Billy said. "I'll go down and see what this guy's story is. No point in you walking clear to the saloon over nothing."

"I appreciate it. If you're not back soon, though, I'm coming after you."

Billy nodded and left.

Jack poured himself a cup of coffee and settled in his chair. The unopened envelope was still on his desk. He picked it up, ran his finger under the seal, and pulled out the contents. He'd been right; it was another drawing. He unfolded it, section by section, gradually revealing the face of a man with a jagged scar down his right cheek. At the top of the face was the word "WANTED" in big square letters. Below the face in the same big square letters were the words "Harold Stone for the murder of Deputy William Knott". Jack threw the paper down, grabbed his rifle, and ran out the door. He'd made it as far as the livery stable when he heard gunshots coming from the saloon. He saw Billy stagger through the wooden doors and collapse in the street. Harold Stone jumped on his horse and was gone before Jack could fire a shot.

Kitty Tee-Shirt

by

J. Baumgartle

I wear five cats to bed every night.
They sit upright, decked in rain gear,
and stare out from the mirror
while I brush my teeth.
The gray, white and tan kitty
has a direct, searching gaze,
full of patience and understanding.
The yellow one, a mystic,
affirms a kind world beyond this one,
lingers on the implications.
The friendly cat in the middle
smiles at whatever's happening
to the left, behind me.
The little gray one
is either young
or innocent of knowing.
The yellow and white striped
confronts protectively
from pale blue eyes.
Behind their backs and mine
a yellow ducky sits,
content. All around them
the weave is giving way,
peripheries shredding,
the shirt becoming a rag.
But galoshes protect their paws
from the puddles in the street,
umbrellas, from the rain,
and because of who they are,
I will never throw them away.

On The Planting of Evidence
by
Marian Allen

A wooden show wagon creaked over the cobbles, drawn by a bulky butter-colored horse. *Festival Players* was painted on every side of the top-heavy conveyance; live flowers and greenery swayed atop the roof. The massive horse stopped and the wagon eased to a halt. Men and women hopped out and let one of the sides down parallel to the ground, propping it with wooden trestles, revealing a threadbare red curtain.

A young man lounged in the tavern's doorway, playing his pipes. His dark eyes flickered over the gathering townsfolk. Who was likely to have coin? Who seemed distracted and careless? He blew a few more notes as he strolled toward the show wagon.

One of the men — a large fellow with a black beard — stopped work, whirled around and pointed to him. "You! With the pipes! Want to be a part of this?"

"No." The piper meant to say no more, but the bearded man seemed to pull the question from him by sheer force of will: "Part of what?"

"Part of what?!" The large man cocked an eyebrow. When he spoke again, he declaimed to everyone in the square. "Jugglers, tumblers, dancers, clowns, and a play in three acts that will stand your hair on end and move your hearts to tears! Just one silver coin, and it's all right here, my friends, right here, tonight, at eventide. Tell your friends!"

The man clapped an arm around the piper's shoulder.

"What's your name, lad?"

"Brady birn Ilka."

"From Kozabir, eh? Wonderful place. They love us there. I'll give you dinner and ten coppers to play for the performance, and a fair share in what the dancers collect at intermission. If it works out tonight, you can come with us. We're heading for Kudasad. Wonderful place. They love us."

Brady had been toying with a swindle based in Kudasad, the capital city. The only thing better than free passage, he reflected, was being paid to go.

"Yes. I'll do it."

"Of course you will! Come and meet everybody." The large man swept a gesture to include himself, two other men and three women. "Silvin, Cristoval, Maida, Sibilla, Odette." The big man slapped his own chest. "I'm Florian. This is Brady, people." He nodded at one of the women. "Sibilla plays for us — lute — but Odette sprained her ankle. Thanks to you, Sibilla can take Odette's place in the dancing. Assuming you can really play."

Brady tootled a scrap of tune and the man seemed satisfied.

"And this firey steed—" Florian waved a hand at the large, placid, beribboned draft horse whose interest was currently occupied by the contents of his nosebag, "—is Lumpkin." He pronounced the name as if it were worthy of a royal stallion.

He appraised the piper, as if visually measuring him for a costume. "You don't act, do you, lad?"

Brady, instantly infected with the stage bug, nearly confessed an ability that would be invaluable in an actor: to shift his shape and the appearance of his clothing. Instead, he shook his head.

Florian sent Sibilla and Brady off to run through some tunes together while the rest of the company set up for the performance and tended to the horse.

"There's an empty storeroom behind The Jolly Magpie," Brady said. "We can practice there."

"Fine, fine." Florian turned his attention elsewhere.

In the storeroom, Brady sized up his companion: darkly pretty, which he liked, but obviously uninterested in him, which he did not like. *Ah, well.*

She opened the worn velvet sack she had brought with her and drew out her lute. For the first time, she smiled.

They played well together. Sibilla asked to see Brady's pipes, and he gave her an introductory lesson in playing them.

As the music ended, so did Sibilla's animation.

Brady's instincts twanged. "Something's wrong. We're going to be traveling together. Is there something about the troupe I ought to know?"

"No. . . . Well, in a way." She sighed. "It's a long story."

"Abbreviate it."

That surprised a chuckle from her. "All right." She paused. "There's a man. Sean." Her face lit up again, briefly.

Inwardly, Brady groaned. If it did bear on the troupe, he needed to hear it, but he dreaded unlocking the secrets of a young maid's heart to get to it.

Sibilla didn't notice the piper's disgust. "We met when we worked for the same cloth merchant in Kudasad."

"You said this had to do with the troupe."

"I'm getting to that! Our plan was to save our pay and join a band of players — see something of the world before we settled down as husband and wife. With our savings, we could afford to leave the company any time and set up house. Have a garden. Sean loves to grow things —"

"I gather it didn't work out." Brady regretted getting her started. Maybe he should play this one performance and then quit. Let whatever trouble this might turn out to be move on without him.

"We joined the Festival Players. Sean had charge of our savings, his and mine. Last week, he came to me and said it had disappeared during the night. He swore he didn't take it, but he said he would always be afraid I thought he did."

"You don't?"

Sibilla's glare was so fierce, Brady flinched.

When she spoke, it was in a flat voice that roused Brady's sympathy in spite of himself. "No, I don't, although everybody else seems to. I trust him. But I couldn't convince him. He left us — me — and went back to the merchant. He said he's going to work there until he can pay back my part of the stolen money."

"When I hear of a man like that —" Brady tucked his pipes into his tunic, " —I'm glad I have no honor."

Sibilla packed her lute and left.

Brady caught up with her. "It was one of the other players who took the money."

She stopped and regarded him through narrowed eyes. "You believe me? You believe him? Why?"

Brady grinned. "If he did it, he would have at least tried to implicate somebody else. Only a completely innocent man would be stupid enough to look that guilty. Since suspicion pointed only to him, whoever really did it is clever and sly. If one of you is that good at covering dishonesty, I need to know who it is. After all, I'm the new addition — anything suspicious that happens from now to six months after I leave will be blamed on me. Anything I get blamed for, I want to be sure I did."

After a long moment, Sibilla walked on.

The show went well that night. Florian paid Brady his coppers and locked the troupe's silver in a heavy metal box built in under the wagon's seat.

The caravan trundled slowly out of town and along the starlit highroad.

Florian drove the wagon, clicking encouragement to the horse, and Odette rode beside him to spare her sprained ankle. The other players, afoot, followed the lanterns fixed to the wagon's tail. Brady walked beside Sibilla, blowing an occasional bit of music.

"How did Odette hurt her ankle?" he asked.

"Twisted it dancing one night."

"Do you trust her?"

Sibilla considered the question. "About as far as I could throw Lumpkin. Why?"

"She palmed some of our coppers after the dancing."

"Are you sure?" She stopped, then had to double-time a few steps to catch up.

"My dear young woman, if anyone knows about palming coins, I do. I palmed some, myself."

"You—!"

"I told you I have no honor. If you want to denounce me for a few pennies when I'm the only one without a share of the troupe's silver, feel free."

Sibilla shook her head, her frown barely visible in the dim light.

After a few paces, Brady spoke again. "You said Sean likes to grow things. Was that garden on top of the wagon his idea?"

"Yes. It's rows of pots around the edge of the top, tied against the trim."

"Who takes care of it?"

"He did, until he left us last week. I do, now."

"How is it doing?"

Sibilla cocked her head, puzzled at his interest. "It's doing well, considering that squirrels got into the pots and dug at the roots."

"When?"

"A few days ago."

"How do you get up to the roof?"

She pointed to a ladder that ran down to within three feet of the ground. "You stand on a wheel to reach the bottom rung."

"If you missed your step on the way down — say, in the dark, when the lamps are out and everybody's asleep — you could hurt yourself, couldn't you?"

"I suppose you could twist your—"

"Now tell me Odette went lame the day the money went missing."

"Yes."

"Now tell me the squirrels had been at your plants the next time you looked."

"Yes."

"Now tell me the squirrels haven't been at the plants since."

Sibilla lunged toward the wagon. Brady caught her and muttered into her ear. "She'll deny it. A twisted ankle isn't proof." Louder, he said, "Watch your step. This is tricky ground."

When the players camped for the night, Sibilla climbed to the roof garden and returned with greens for the stew pot.

"That isn't all I harvested up there," she told Brady, her eyes flashing rage. "Our money — every coin of it — was divided among the pots. That proves who the thief is. If Sean had stolen the money, he'd have taken it with him."

"So Sean is innocent, but it doesn't prove that Odette is guilty."

Sibilla growled in exasperation. "Then how do we prove it?"

"We?"

"You said you believe me. Doesn't that make you part of 'we'?"

Well, no. But he rather liked his fellow musician, and he had a grudge against Odette, who had stolen some of the coppers he considered his rightful plunder.

"She'll have to confess."

Sibilla snorted. "I can't imagine that."

"It will happen." When Sibilla's disbelief refused to melt before his assurance, he said, "In three more days, we'll be in Kudasad. Odette will confess after the show there. But you have to help."

"What do I do?"

"Practice the pipes."

Florian and his players were very small fry in the capital, and could only rent a corner of a minor square. Still, they had a good show, and enough copper and silver came in to make the performance worthwhile. Even Lumpkin benefited, with a stall in a nearby livery stable.

After the play, an elderly gentleman, elegantly attired, approached Odette.

"Dear lady, I've delighted in watching you dance before. Why have I been denied the pleasure tonight?"

"I hurt my ankle." She raised her hem coquettishly. "But it's nearly well."

"Poor, brave lady! Let me treat you to dinner across the way. You will do me the honor?"

He gave her his arm and led her across the cobbles and into the brightly lit inn.

Shortly thereafter, Brady returned from an unnamed errand. "Time for practice," he said to Sibilla, "I on your lute and you on my pipes."

The other players set up a brazier beside the wagon and sat around the blaze on campstools, passing a bottle of wine and savoring performances past. From the caravan came inexpert strumming on Sibilla's lute, echoed with more or less accuracy on the pipes.

A thump and a muffled curse from the front of the wagon brought Florian and the others to their feet.

"Silvin and Maida — go around that way. Cristoval — come with me."

They made out the figure of Odette in the shadows by the strongbox.

Florian loomed over her. "What do you think you're doing?"

"I'm only taking what's mine." Odette clutched a moneybag. "If it weren't for me, this troupe would attract nothing but riff-raff. It's my work that brings us silver, and I get no more for my share than the others. That isn't fair, and I'm tired of it."

Florian spoke quietly. "Give it back."

"I won't!" Odette's shout was shockingly loud.

The curtain slid aside in the wagon's front window and Sibilla leaned out. "What's going on?"

By the time the players, dazzled by the sudden light, knew what was happening, Odette was gone. They had barely begun to lay blame for her escape when an enraged woman thrust herself into the group.

"Now what?" she snarled.

It was Odette.

Cristoval and Silvin grasped her wrists and held her as she writhed and cursed.

This time, Florian was not quiet. "WHERE IS IT?"

"Where is what?"

"The money!"

"What money?"

Sibilla made a noise of outrage. "We know you for a thief. You can stop pretending."

Florian favored direct simplicity. "Give it back, or I'll call a constable."

Odette tried to twist free, but the men held her fast. "All right! I'll tell you where it is, but someone else will have to get it."

"Tell me, then."

"I buried it in the pots on the roof."

"What roof?"

Odette looked at Florian as if he were a fool. "The wagon roof. The big lummox slept like the dead. I took the money and buried it in his own precious plants, but I slipped on the way down and hurt myself and had to say I'd done it dancing."

"What are you talking about?"

Sibilla's voice was rich with satisfaction. "She's talking about the money she stole from Sean."

Florian was a man who knew how to stick to the point. "Where

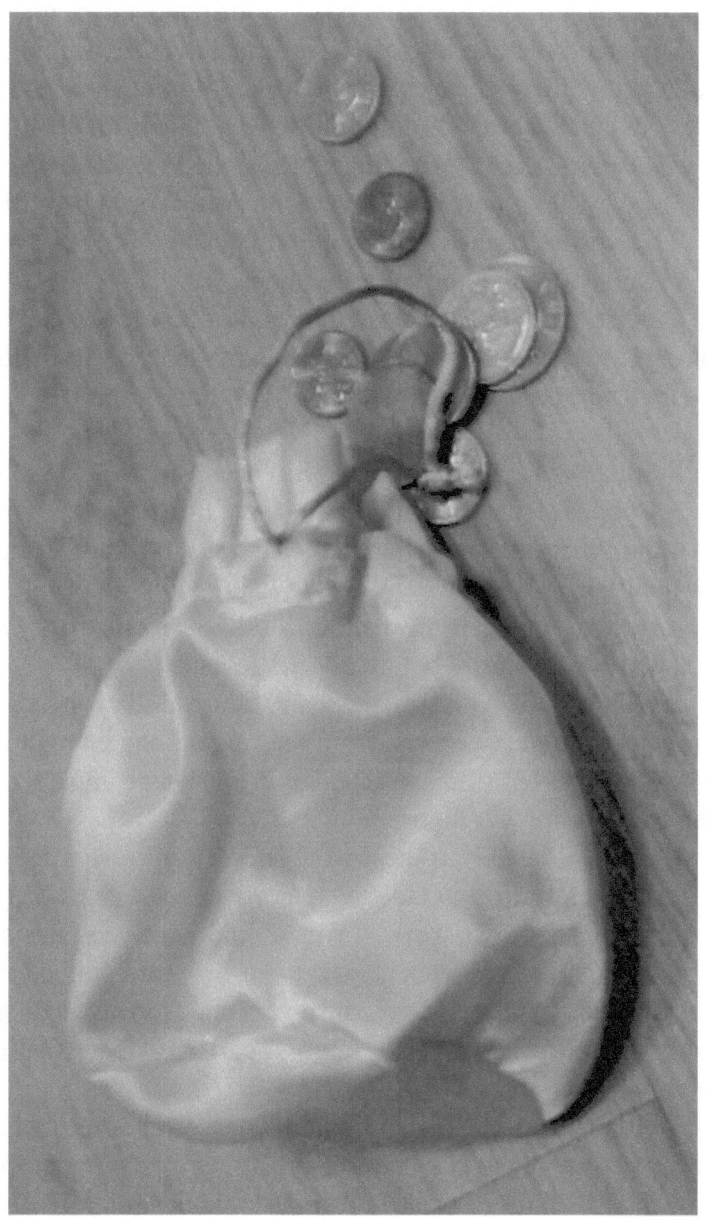

is the troupe's money?"

Odette tried again to pull free. "I don't have the troupe's money!"

Florian unlocked the strongbox . . . and removed the moneybag inside. He spread the bag into a circle, turned over the shining coins with satisfaction, tied the bag shut and locked it safely away. "Let her go." He looked at Sibilla. "I don't know what this is all about, but it seems we owe your Sean an apology." He smiled ruefully. "I suppose we'll be looking for a new lute player tomorrow. You'll be off to find him, eh? No chance of the two of you joining us again?"

"I think our traveling days are done."

Brady shouldered a place in the window beside Sibilla. "You'll be looking for a new piper, too. This is as far as I go. And you'll be looking for a new dancer. Odette just left. This time, I don't think she'll come back."

Florian, Maida, Cristoval, and Silvin considered Odette's final departure a good riddance and a welcome simplification, removing the burden of puzzling out her earlier theft-that-wasn't-a-theft. They went back to their wine.

Inside the wagon, Brady handed Sibilla the moneybag "Odette" had clutched so vigorously before her first escape.

Sibilla took it with a triumphant flourish. "I wondered how you were going to get her away from the wagon long enough for the trick to work. It was as simple as changing your shape into a flattering old man and offering her dinner."

"Anyone as greedy as she is would never turn down a free meal." Brady shifted his form into Odette's elderly devotee for a heartbeat, then returned to his own shape. "You should have seen her simper when I excused myself to fetch her a present." He caricatured Odette's gratified avarice. "As for you, you did a very good job pretending to be both of us in here while I performed the part of Odette stealing the troupe's moneybag."

Sibilla chuckled. "I wish I could have seen her face when her beau never returned and she had to pay for her own dinner. She was furious when she showed up. Too furious to think straight."

The musicians shared wicked grins.

Sibilla hefted her moneybag. "You had no trouble slipping back in here unnoticed?"

On The Planting of Evidence

"With Florian and the real Odette bellowing at the front of the wagon? None at all." Brady sighed. "We work well together. Too bad you're honest. Besides, like your Sean, you're too trusting."

"You confided your shape-shifting secret to me, and you call me too trusting?"

"You gave me your moneybag to use as a prop. That wasn't wise."

Sibilla untied the purse's strings and opened it. It was filled with small, flat stones.

"But — " Brady gaped. "I didn't — I said you could trust me, and—"

"Trust you?" Sibilla dug into the bottom of her lute sack and extracted another bag — one which clinked as she shook it. "When you told me yourself you have no honor?"

Diamond Rose

By

Teddi Robinson

I was sitting in the swing, on the porch, thinking about my six granddaughters when I saw Terry, my favorite, coming up the walk. *I can't believe that she's 15 years old. It seems like it was only yesterday I watched her dance the role of Clara in 'The Nutcracker'. Just look at her long black hair and her build. Yes, she does look like a ballet dancer. Maybe she'll become one.*

Joining me, Terry said, "Grandma, I think I can be honest with you about a decision that I need to make."

"Honey, you can tell me anything and I'll try to be helpful."

"Good, because I have the opportunity to join one of two groups of girls at school. The one group goes to church, takes part in school activities, and . . . well . . . they're nice, but they're pretty boring. The kids in the other group don't go to church, ignore school activites, and anything for fun is okay. I have friends in both groups, but I can't belong to both. I need you to help me decide."

"Honey, everyone makes this choice at some point in their life. I had to make that decision when I was about your age."

"I know, you're going to tell me all about your accomplishments and how it would have been a lot different if you had gone with the other group."

"No, I'm going to tell you a story about a girl named Diamond Rose."

"Who is Diamond Rose and why was she called that?"

"They named her Rose Ann when she was born. The Rose after her grandmother and the Ann after her mother. When Rose was in the 7th grade, her aunt started sending her the magazine 'Seventeen'. Rose wanted to be as sophisticated as the models. She tried to give the impression that everything she owned was expensive. This wasn't easy: no one had any money during the Depression, let alone her family.

"Her mother was an expert seamstress, though, and made the most beautiful dresses out of the printed cotton from feed sacks. Rose would show up in hose, heels, and a beautiful corsage for all school activities, and the kids started calling her Diamond Rose.

"She was always in the school plays and on the honor roll. Her parents were so proud. Things changed when she entered High School. More classes and not with the same teacher, more students and activities.

"Rose had a couple of classes with Sue. Sue was always laughing and talking about the exciting weekends that she and her friends, Randy, Paul, and John enjoyed. It sounded like a lot of fun and Rose asked if she could go with them sometime. At first they would go to the teen dances or the movies. The guys were smart, neat, and fun. Randy's dad always kept 4 or 5 cases of beer at home.

"One evening Randy said. 'Let's go by my house and I'll get some of dad's beer.'

"Rose protested but was out-voted. They didn't get drunk that night but one bottle of beer a night wasn't enough and soon they were getting drunk. Then it was driving around town, running red lights and breaking the speed limit, yelling at people, trespassing on other people's land, and taking yard decorations—kid stuff, mostly. But one evening the group was pretty high on beer and out of money.

Someone suggested, 'Let's rob a service station.'

"Everyone thought that was a great idea. Randy had a gun. He enjoyed target shooting every chance he got. No one would get hurt, but the gun would make the robbery a success.

"It didn't go as planned. The station attendant also had a gun. Shots were fired and the attendant was wounded. Rose was driving the getaway car."

Terry's eyes were wide, and I could see she had been imagining herself on a spree that went wrong. "Gee, they were lucky that the service attendant wasn't killed. Weren't they? Even if I did run with the wild crowd, I'd never do that."

"Honey, when you run with a wild crowd, you do what they do on the spur of the moment. However, their appetite for the wild life was not satisfied. They robbed more stores and service stations. They decided to rob a bank."

"Oh, no!"

"Oh, yes. The bank had the new security button that a clerk could push to notify the police that a robbery was in progress. All five were caught before they could make their getaway."

"But not Rose."

"Rose, too. Since this was her first *known* offense, she was sentenced to prison for five years. She didn't like it."

"I guess not. I wish she'd escaped."

"Well, I'll tell you something." I leaned forward and said, in a confidential murmur, "She did."

Terry was still such a child. Her eyes shone with delighted relief.

I sat back and said, "That was a long time ago and she was never caught. She ran from town to town and state to state, always afraid of being recognized and having to go back to prison. She always worked in restaurants, from dishwasher to cook. Finally a customer noticed how pretty she was. He offered her a job as a dance hall girl. That was where she met the love of her life."

"Dance hall girl? Like in Westerns?"

I laughed. "No. This was a place where people came to dance. Some men didn't have partners, so the dance halls hired girls. About 30 or 40 of them would all line up against a wall. The men were charged 10 cents a ticket, and they got to choose the girl they wanted to dance with. One ticket entitled them to one dance.

"Carl wasn't handsome. In fact, he didn't have a face, just a nose. That nose was the only thing any of the girls saw. Everyone was hoping Carl would dance with someone else, not them. Well, the first dance he choose a cute, petite brunette. The rest of the girls sighed a breath of relief. Then he chose Rose. And talk about a dancer! He was graceful, knew all the latest steps, and was a wonderful conversationalist. Of course, he danced with Rose the rest of the evening. He told her later that he had spotted her as he was buying the tickets, but he thought she would refuse to dance with him, because she was so pretty. The girls were not allowed to turn down a dance at any time, but that was the reason he gave for choosing the brunette. I think Rose fell in love with him that night. He came every night and always bought all her dance tickets.

"Rose was very thrilled when Carl asked her to marry him, but was in quite a state. She didn't want him to know about her past. She never discussed her past with anyone except to tell Carl that she had moved around a lot, she was an only child, and her parents were dead.

"The downside was, Rose had to continue to look over her

shoulder her entire life, always afraid that someone would recognize her, turn her in—or, worse, try to blackmail her. The statute of limitation doesn't run out for a jail break, so she still feels threatened by strangers. Can you imagine how much fun you would get from your life if you had to look over your shoulder all the time?"

Terry's mouth dropped open, as something in my face gave me away. "Why, *you're* Diamond Rose, aren't you? This story is about you. Isn't it?"

"Yes. You've guessed my secret. The family doesn't know and they probably wouldn't believe it after so many years of respectability. Please don't tell them. Okay?"

"You mean you never told my mother or anyone?"

"No. My relationship with your mother wasn't a good one. When she wanted to do things I didn't approve of, I would tell her no. If she tried to question my decision. . . . I would say, "You can't, because I said so.' I just couldn't tell her what I've told you today."

Terry jumped up and gave me a big hug. "Your secret is safe with me, and now I know why you keep telling me to choose my friends with care. I think I'll stay with the BORING group. At least I won't get into trouble with them." She hugged me again. "I love you, Diamond Rose."

"And I love you."

My Father Was
by
Ardis Moonlight

Clouds like people asleep floated in heavy dark outside the plane—
where to look, what to think.
The man next to me smoked the air with cigarettes, inane questions—
what to say, what to do.

My dad was a new Ford every year caressing two-lane roads
   to Beaver Dam, Caneyville, Cave City,
   Glasgow, Columbia, Bowling Green,
   talking cultivators, combines, tractors,
   bringing home corn, tomatoes, green beans,
      sometimes watermelon,
   not the pint of whiskey under the driver's seat.

My dad was a golf club swinging sweat on weekends
   over eighteen holes, hills, pulling a cart of metal,
   bringing home silver chalices engraved,
   filming daughters becoming women leaving trails in the club pool,
      reversing the bobbing caps and strokes
   into dives, standing at the edge, the diving board.

My father was a ringside, wing-backed chair in a smoky living room
   lit by quiet athletes crowding the television.
   Licking a cigar, biting off the end, he'd light the brief fragrance,
      concentrating fiercely on each sport,
      radio chatter his companion.

He had a daughter who couldn't be a son,
      but caught passes, kicked elliptical shapes into the sun.
   He didn't know a daughter who became a golfer,
      playing more than he, encouraging a grandson.
   He combed tangles of hair for the youngest, tangling her heart.

My father was a sofa drinking novels, magazines, newspapers *every
night*—
     the first time in eighteen years.
  Daughters used to fish sticks, chicken pot pies,
  "I Love Lucy", "The Mickey Mouse Club",
  a mother eating and reading in the kitchen,
     faced each other around a table,
     no one knew what to do or say.
  Tension as thick as the beef he grilled,
  Mother confided divorce—
     but if he just left.

My father was a car again, a used model,
     selling knick knacks in small Kentucky towns.
     In Princeton, his engine stopped.

*Clouds like people asleep floated in heavy dark outside the plane—
     where to look, what to think.
     The man next to me smoked the air with cigarettes, inane
questions—
     what to say, what to do.*

Contributors

The Southern Indiana Writers Group has been more-or-less together since 1992. We began meeting monthly in a conference room in a local hospital. We now meet weekly to exchange information and expertise on everything from computers to poetry. The group also serves as a critique forum (in the same sense that a pack of wolves serves as food critics). Membership is limited, but visitors are welcome, and have been known to fit in so well they become members against their better judgment.

Bonnie Abraham After twenty-five plus years of writing letters disqualifying people from Unemployment Benefits, she retired in order to write something more pleasant. She writes short stories (many with Biblical themes), poetry and devotionals. Currently, she resides in Corydon with her mother's ghost.

Marian Allen lives in a big house in a little wood, which is not the only difference between Allen and Laura Ingels Wilder. She has published stories in print and on-line magazines, including Marion Zimmer Bradley's FANTASY Magazine, The Phone Book, PanGaia and Oceans of the Mind.

Jeannine Baumgartle writes poetry and fiction. Her work has appeared in publications such as *Green Meadow Press*, *Flying Island, Literally*, and Studio: *A Journal for Christians Writing* and won a residency for poetry at the Mary Anderson Center for the Arts . She and her husband live in the small town of Crandall.

Ginny Fleming considers herself to be foremost a screenwriter, as this is her favorite media. Because nobody thought to tell her she couldn't, after optioning 3 scripts for the unsold ensemble sitcom *"Tia"* (any producers reading this?), Fleming dived head-first into the shark-infested mulligan stew (How's that for mixing metaphors?) that is Hollywood scriptwriting. Her romantic comedy scripts can be previewed at *The Spec Script Library*, *Writer's Market*, and *Writers.Net*.

Fleming's take on hysterical fantasy (funny, that is), a novel she likes to call *Dragonsayver* (when she's not calling it Marvin), is a "Shrek-like" novel just begging to be made into an animated film (Fleming wonders if she should shove a tin cup in its hand and drop it on a busy intersection....). Besides her annual contribution to SIW anthology and a brief appearance in the Louisville Courier-Journal, Fleming is busy finding a home for *Keys of Illusion*, a Romantic/Suspense novel filled with magic, scuba, fantasy, a bunch of lavender stuff and little bit of sex. Multiple scripts are always in the works whenever Fleming manages to "channel" Jimmy Buffett, her "Muse" (Yeah, she knows Jimmy's not dead — Hopes for his continued good health, in fact — That just makes him easier to channel).

Joanna Foreman writes short fiction and slice-of-life vignettes. Her first collection of short stories, *Ghosts of Interstate 65,* was published in January, 2008. She is currently working on her first novel which is set along the River Walk in San Antonio, Texas. Her frequent weekend getaways to the River Walk keep her in touch with the imaginary characters living there. Above all, Joanna's first priority is family, although she occasionally experiences sudden urges to move to the moon for escape purposes. Her ten-year-old granddaughter advises her to take her cell phone so she can be kept abreast of the family's shenanigans while she is gone. Joanna and her husband Craig married barefooted on St. Augustine Beach in 2001. They built a modest home smack-dab in the middle of two wooded acres and will live happily ever after.

T Lee Harris is a writer and illustrator who has been a lover of mystery and the detective genre since discovering books. A graduate of Indiana University with a Bachelor of Fine Arts, T has been involved with radio production, game design, comic books and desktop publishing. Interests include participation in the Society for Creative Anachronism and Renaissance Faires, tailoring authentic costuming for re-enactors and playing online roleplaying games. Several novels are in progress featuring Sitehuti and Nefer-Djenou-Bastet, Josh Katzen and a series set in ninth century Ireland. Work has appeared in print and online venues including mystericale.com and Cat Tales.

Contributors

Joy Kirchgessner lives in Corydon with her husband, Mike. Her interests are too vast to list on this page. She's a long time business woman of Corydon, and artist, whose nature paintings have been accepted into prestigious shows, photographer, whose photographs have joined her illustrations in our anthologies, equestrian, who enjoys trail rides, amateur archaeologist, who enjoys rock hunting and exploring new worlds—give her a chemistry set and a laboratory and she'd try to split atoms. Many years ago, Southern Indiana Writers tied her to a computer and wonderful stories blossomed from Kirchgessner's many interests. So now, she must add accomplished writer to that long, long list. She even has a novel or two in the early stages.

Glenda Mills resides in New Albany, Indiana with her husband and youngest son. She has a daughter and a son who no longer live at home and one grandchild. When she is not busy homemaking, homeschooling, attending soccer games, running the family taxi service, or volunteering at her church, she writes fiction, nonfiction, and poetry. She looks forward to the day when a person can actually be in two places at once.

Ardis Moonlight quite naturally is a fan of the moon and stars, and finally can see it all in Harrison County, a plus after 32 years in Louisville! A poet with poems published in several issues of "Calliope", an anthology published yearly by Women Who Write, she is also trying her imagination with short stories, and....gasp...considering a novel!

Teddi Robinson has taken several creative writing classes and has (With a lot of encouragement) just published her first book, *The Meddlers*. She is currently at work polishing the sequel for publication before the end of 2008.

Previous Publications by Southern Indiana Writers

Indian Creek Anthology
Ghost Writers
Christmas Bizarre
Dragon: Our Tales
Grounds for Suspicion
2000 Tales
Way Out West
Unbridled Lust
There's Something Under the Bedtime Stories
Novel Ingredients
Write of Passage
Off the Rack
Beastly Tales
It's Always Something
Most Wanted

Coming Soon:

FUTURE
PERFECT
(TENSE IN SPACE)

Visit our web site for excerpts of previous publications
and availability information:

http://southernindianawriters.com